Her Viking Saviour

Lore & Love Trilogy
Book 1

Steffy Smith

Steffy Smith Books

First published in Australia in 2024 by Steffy Smith Books

Edited by Juicy Details Romance Editing, 2024

Cover design by GM Cover Designs

Formatted by Duncan Swindells @ ELDP

A catalogue record for this book is available from the National Library of Australia.

E-book ISBN: 978-0-6454448-8-9

Paperback ISBN: 978-0-6454448-9-6

This one is for you, my readers.

"It is very beautiful. It almost does not seem real."

Any ire in her tone had vanished and he could only hear awe at the imagery before them. Having been to Northumbria, he tried to see it through her fresh eyes. He knew these sights differed vastly from her homeland.

"We have many long houses, many trade fronts. I am very proud of what my people have built over years of hard labour." She nodded. They were close enough to see the edge of the town that lay beyond the piers where the ships docked.

"Have you thought any more about what you might do here?" he asked her.

"I have been thinking, though I am still unsure."

Her posture was tense again, her voice guarded.

"Do not worry, Wynflaed. I think I know what you can do here."

Prologue

Odin tapped his foot impatiently inside the root of Yggdrasil while he waited for the Norns to acknowledge his presence. He could not help a wry smile at their indifference, the only ones who could and did treat him so. They were ancient but still youthful, all-knowing but uncaring, as was their nature.

Gives me a good dose of humility at least.

He rolled his eye at the thought. Patience was not one of his virtues. This was an earthy space. Dirt and grass, wood and stone. He breathed the scent in deeply, so pure and untouched by any other living realm.

Give me the smell of mead, battle sweat, and the heady aroma of a woman.

More moments passed and still they did not speak to him, nor even look at him, so he watched them. Urd stared blankly at her hands and Skuld watched Urd. Verdandi tended a large pot over a roaring fire, humming tunelessly to herself. To think that these three held the fate of the worlds at their fingertips, for gods and mortals alike. Odin shook his head in disbelief as he always did when he paid a visit to the Norns. He cleared his throat since the tapping of his foot had gone unnoticed.

"Ah, Odin," Urd spoke, but her gaze was still on her hands, her silvery blonde hair curtaining her expression. "We have not forgotten you. Time passes differently for us."

They always reminded him of this. That, while he was a god–the God of all gods, realms, and all who dwell in them—his authority did not include the Nornir. The fact that he had been addressed meant he was getting somewhere.

"Of course, Urd, forgive me. It is an honour just to be in the presence of the wise and fated," he said with a bow.

He knew this pleased Skuld for she saw everything, even if her gaze was directed at Urd. Now she turned to him, and he gave her his most charming grin. Skuld was the most attractive of the Norns, though he knew better than to attempt to seduce her.

"You come seeking guidance for one of your warriors." It was a statement rather than a question, her tone a soft purr.

"You are unsure what to tell him when he calls on you for advice about his path. You want to know his fate," Verdandi said.

"Torben Ulfson is currently in Mercia, and I foresee him becoming sickened by the battles and bloodshed. He is a man capable of many things, but he is one of the most fierce and talented warriors I have seen."

"You are correct, Odin. There are many paths Torben "Hel-Bringer" Ulfson could walk. You are also right that he tires of the pillaging, destructive ways of the Viking; the bloodshed of men, women and children. If he stays in abroad, in time, he will become a shadow of his former self. If he returns home to lead and care for his people, he will still honour you by living the way of the Norse. He will be ready and able to defend his lands in Midgard, in your name."

Odin nodded, soaking in the words. Torben had been calling to him, asking for Odin's wisdom, a sign. And now

Odin could give him one. There was good in Torben's heart, a rarity in this time.

"My thanks, Urd, Skuld, and Verdandi—your wisdom leaves me much to contemplate."

Chapter One

10 years later

Wynflaed shed her filthy, ragged clothing and stepped into the chilly stream in this unchosen foreign land. All she could see were tall trees and shrubbery with no signs of human life. Not even an animal scurrying away. After the torturous boat journey surrounded by a growing filth and stench, the cold, biting water was a warm welcome. Exhausted, she could muster no shame at her nudity but she was still thankful that her captors were at a slight distance, uninterested in watching them all bathe. She had no energy for modesty. Wynflaed lowered herself into the clear depths and squeezed her eyes tight as recent tumultuous events replayed in her mind.

Word had been sent that her father was dying, and she had been allowed to travel back to the small village in Northumbria where she had been born. The visit had been brief, and her father had asked her forgiveness for choosing a life of servitude as the handmaiden to the eldest daughter of a wealthy nobleman over arranging for her to marry. The icy water sluiced over her skin, and she blocked out the noises trying to invade her thoughts. Birds trilled and water burbled, but these peaceful, everyday sounds were broken by the harsh syllables of the Viking tongue. She heard some familiar words scattered throughout their speech, which suggested their captors could speak to them as equals, but she knew keeping the prisoners in the dark was another way to keep them scared. She kept hearing the word *thrall* and knew it meant slave. Giving her head a shake, she turned her thoughts back to the last moments she had spent with her father.

Wynflaed had given him her forgiveness with no regret. In truth, she would have been worse off if another path had been chosen for her. As a handmaiden in a wealthy household, she had been treated well. She had been fed, clothed, and housed and she had observed, and at times participated in, her mistress's learnings and activities. If she had been married to a serf her life could have proven harsh, so she held her father's hand tightly as he drew his last breath and freely gave her blessings upon his soul for all eternity. She was not one to brood and curse unless sorely provoked, which her life experiences had not given her much cause for so far.

Wynflaed *did* curse the events that had led her to be bathing in these frigid waters. As her party—herself, two guards and Hilde, an older female servant—had travelled back through Northumbria, they had crossed paths with a marauding band of heathen Vikings. Raiding parties were always a concern travelling through these lands, but it had been some time since she had heard of one close to home. The barbarians had made short work of the outnumbered guards and had abducted herself and Hilde, to whom Wynflaed owed a debt of gratitude.

When Hilde had spotted the marauders in the distance, she had made the sign of the cross, pulled off Wynflaed's wimple, thrown it to the ground, and taken a dagger to her curly, long, black hair. Wynflaed, looking in shock at the Vikings in the distance who had now spied them, had not even flinched as her hair fell to the ground. She could see no possibility of escape and had frozen, not knowing whether they should fight or set flight. The irony had not been lost on her that her journey to give her father absolution before death had led her to meet death itself.

And no wonder I am of little faith, she thought with a shake of her head.

"Come now, child, before they see you up close. You are very fair, and we need to make you less so."

Wynflaed had nodded to Hilde as the guards had bravely taken an offensive position and the Vikings drew nearer. The Vikings had laughed and had not quickened their steps as they approached in a casual manner. Their cockiness and lazy approach had angered her, as though they knew there was no way they could lose to these helpless serfs, just two men and two women. Hilde had smudged dirt all over Wynflaed's face and rubbed a piece of fish they had intended for their repast over her clothes. *Thank God*, she had thought, as the Vikings paid no attention to her after a once-over glance at her form except to note she would fetch a price. A price, as if she were a goat or chicken to be sold at the market. Not a living breathing human such as they.

The ship's journey had seemed endless as the salty waves crashed relentlessly against the hull of the boat. The captives had huddled together on the ship, with no small comforts or privacy, despite their growing stench. They had stayed huddled together in cold and fear as their captors rowed, drank, and sang songs they could not understand. The fear had slowly left Wynflaed, and anger had started to settle in. Before this, she had never questioned her lot in life, simple as it was. But this was different, something inside her had raged and quaked at the injustice, wrought upon them by these Vikings that seemed to fall from the sky onto her home soil as habitually as the rain.

Rising out of the water, she used her hands to scrub every

inch of her body and hair, not knowing when she would next be afforded such a luxury. Even with no soap, the water still worked wonders, though it left her flesh momentarily revealed. The dirt and fish stink Hilde had used to mask her had reached the end of its usefulness. There was no escaping *them*. She stepped onto the bank and looked around at her fellow captives she had met on the ship. They had their arms wrapped around their shivering bodies and Wynflaed scanned the group for Hilde. She found her with Cynewin and Cola. Both younger than her and terrified, they had barely said a word. The other three captives were older men, and from their appearance had been serfs, not warriors. They would have had no way of fighting these Vikings and escaping. Wynflaed thought of the guards with sadness and wondered what would have been worse for them: to be dead back on home soil— becoming one with the dirt—or to be here, captured and ready to be sold.

Her morbid thoughts were broken when a rough linen shift was thrust at her chest. She looked up and came eye to eye with one of her captors who looked her up and down with a suspicious yet appreciative gleam in his eyes that soured her stomach. She was no longer in her filthy and smelly disguise and the loss of her crowning glory seemed of no import to his lust. She quickly donned it, putting a layer of protection between her body and his beady eyes. His leer held ill intent and she would rather die than allow him to touch her.

"Do not get any ideas, Hakkan. She is for sale and not for you." The one she had assumed was their leader laughed and the rest of his men laughed with him. The leader was a very large man who reminded her of a bear. He was always smiling and laughing but she had noticed it never reached his small, dark eyes. He held no kindness in his heart. What man who dealt in the trade of human flesh could?

The one named Hakkan grinned at her as if he expected

her to laugh and shoved her forward to huddle with the others. All she could do was grit her teeth and right herself. She stood tall and stiffened her spine, a simple but defiant act. Not that it would do much. Finding Hilde, she stood close to the shivering woman and waited to see what would happen next. Despite their open surroundings, she felt like she was standing in a tiny room with the walls closing in. She was afraid, helpless, and, most of all, enraged at these filthy beasts, who treated them as if they were animals to be sold at market.

I must do something. But what?

Chapter Two

Torben Ulfson stared out across the hordes of people who had travelled here from all around the world. He stood so tall, even by Norse standards, that he had not yet seen a person today that equalled his height, and it gave him a good view of the thriving hive. The popular centre of the trade route that ran through Kyivan Rus held value for traders and barterers alike. The exotic blend of foreign food odours and noise was never a dull experience. You needed discipline to ensure you did not lose yourself in the curiosities. This was never an issue for Torben, he had blade-sharp senses that had served him well in battle and now in trade.

This year, he had brought heavy furs and pelts, expertly crafted axes, and salted skrei, a codfish unique to the seas of his homeland. The bear and wolf pelts were very popular. He had men that travelled to the coldest parts of the north to hunt the huge white bears. It took brave men to pursue these bears, enormous in size and ferocious in temper, and few would take on the challenge. Those who did faced near-certain odds of death. But his men had hunted them for years. Fathers passed knowledge to their sons about how to best these beasts. To beat them you had to know them, to know their habits, weaknesses, and strengths. The yellowish-white bear pelts were always the first to go. When he and his ships sailed up to the dock, the people knew to start lining up.

But it was not just he who brought sought-after goods. From the East, there were silks, spices, jewels, and exotic animals—he spent little on these goods, buying silk and spice sparingly if there was a need. Sometimes he came across other textiles and the clothes makers back home eagerly put them to use. From the West came weapons and tools, things he could trade for. He had no desire to go to battle, but he believed in being prepared. He kept a well-stocked arsenal of swords, axes, arrowheads, and spears, in case the need ever arose to defend his settlement. He would only draw a blade to defend, not attack. Senseless bloodshed and brutality were not the path he wanted for himself and his people.

Of course, there was another trade—the one he despised the most—the trade of humans. Slaves. Thralls. This despicable trade was popular and he avoided these stalls at all costs or he would intervene. It was an unfortunate truth of the world, and he could only hope that one day it would be abolished for good. He did not believe human life should have a price.

As a seasoned warrior, Torben had seen and brought death and destruction to many men. But that was war. When you pick up a weapon to face your enemy you must accept that this may be the day you die. He never believed the spoils of war included humans, but many—including his Viking brethren —did, and used them as personal slaves or profited from the indentured life they sold them into.

Torben scanned the crowd, looking for any signs of discontent. He always felt edgy in foreign lands and liked to do his business and leave. He was intrigued by the languages he overheard and how men from all over the seas, speaking different tongues, were able to strike a deal. He had used his time raiding from Mercia to Wessex to learn their language and during other raids and trading had picked up Frankish and the language of the Rus, a Norse dialect. He found this knowledge invaluable, and believed if everyone could share speech there would be more understanding and less animosity.

He took a moment to listen more closely and heard an accent he didn't quite recognise. He spied two men, their skin many shades darker than his own, deep in conversation. Their tone was melodic, and he could tell from their smiles and enthusiastic hand gestures that they spoke of something that brought them joy. Scanning the crowd again, he saw more animated conversations, but of a different tenor. These hand gestures spoke of heated bartering and haggling, and he said a silent thanks his cousin Leif handled that side of the trade.

"You are always so serious in expression, Torben. We are in the land of luxury and mysterious delights for a short time, why not enjoy ourselves?" said his younger brother Ragnav with a grin. Torben had not realised he had been watching his pensive observations. He stood only an inch shorter than Torben and, while they shared the same piercing blue eyes, Ragnav was dark-haired while he was fair. Their mother liked to say that Torben had sapped all the seriousness out of her womb and by the time Ragnav came along there was none to share. Their father liked to joke their hair colour was wrong, as Torben's fair hair suited Ragnav's disposition better than his own darker, broodier nature.

He followed his brother's line of sight as Ragnav winked provocatively. The object of his flirtation was a tanned beauty throwing sultry looks their way. She clearly had an eye for good coin and made no secret of her invitation. Rolling his eyes, he clapped loudly in front of Ragnav's face to gain his attention. Ragnav gave a good-natured shrug and bowed mockingly to Torben.

"You have my attention, my wise and celibate brother."

Torben rolled his eyes. Again.

"Follow me, I want to see who else is trading goods like ours."

Torben wanted to keep their wealth strong through trade, not just raiding, and he took any opportunity to scout out potential competition. As they moved through the large crowd, he wrinkled his nose at the odour of unwashed bodies that wafted through the stagnant air. Suddenly, he heard a scream and instinctively moved his hand to the great axe at his hip. His senses tingled with danger, and he searched intently for the source.

He saw a crowd forming in the distance and moved closer to investigate. Soon he sighted a group of fellow Northmen. Viking warriors. He could tell by their stance and heavy weaponry they were not peaceful traders. They stood around a huddled group of pale people in linen shifts that he identified straightaway as Saxons. They looked ragged and ill-treated. Torben had spent time in Jorvik, Mercia, Northumbria, raiding and fighting with his father, and had come to learn these people, their language, and their customs. He had found them to be mild-mannered people, though rightly angered at the invasion of their homeland.

He was surprised when a young woman with oddly-shorn raven-coloured hair stood in front of another woman and pushed one of the Viking men with all her might. The man did not budge an inch, just laughed in her face. The silly girl did not give up and sprang up on her toes to slap him across the face. Her hand connected and he howled, either in pain as one of her fingernails scratched him, or in shame as the watching crowd laughed. He unsheathed a dagger at his belt and Torben saw her look of rage fade to fear, though her stance was still defiant, and he was unable to stop himself from intervening.

"Put down your weapon."

His voice was hard, but he spoke the words evenly and calmly. It was a tone that allowed no disobedience and the opposing Viking obeyed but eyed him furiously.

"Who in Hel are you to give me an order?" the Viking roared, his dagger now lowered.

"I am Torben Ulfson," he said without any rancour. He held no feeling for this man, knowing he raised his voice in pride and not in challenge. The man raised a quizzical brow as if he recognized the name. Before Torben could speak any further, another man stepped forward and spoke.

"Ahh, Haakan, we have the infamous Torben "Hel-Bringer" gracing our lowly presence," said a familiar voice and he turned to meet the stare of Guthred.

Chapter Three

Wynflaed shivered, not from cold but from trepidation, as the adrenaline slowly left her body after her brash actions. She had never acted on an instinct so strong as the one she felt to defend Hilde. Poor Hilde had tripped and fallen, and when she had tried to stand up, the brute Haakan had kicked her hard in the abdomen. Wynflaed was sure he had caused a serious injury and the idea of Hilde suffering after trying to protect her was unbearable. The consequences of her challenge did not register until the sharp blade stared her in the face. She must have seemed addled to the crowd as she looked to and fro between Haakan and this new Viking. Torben the Hel-Bringer. She knew Hel was associated with the heathen afterlife, so she could only assume this man brought about death.

What she did not understand was the interest he had in saving her life.

He was taller than any man here, fair-haired with the bluest eyes she had ever seen. Even with the distance between them, she could see the colour as vibrantly as if she stood next to him. When he turned towards the man that had named him, she thought she saw a muscle twitch in his jaw. Otherwise, he showed no emotion. He was a true stoic and she welcomed his interruption, whatever his motivation.

"Guthred. It has been an age since we saw each other," he replied calmly. His voice was deep and melodic, sending a tingle down her spine.

"Indeed, it has been, my old friend. And young Ragnav, look how you have grown! Almost as tall as Torben." Guthred continued like they were old friends meeting in a more pleasant circumstance than this violent spectacle.

Ragnav smiled and nodded his head but stayed by Torben's side in a defensive stance. Wynflaed spied his hand resting near the hilt of a sword. Guthred grinned, apparently enjoying the tension.

"Come now, Torben. Tell me what is wrong so we can continue with our day."

"People from all over come here for trade, not for bloodshed. Why is your man treating a woman so?" he replied in an even tone.

Wynflaed felt a rush of gratitude for the handsome stranger coming to her defence and gave Torben a small smile. She saw his eyes crinkle slightly as if he wanted to smile in return and felt an odd flutter in her stomach.

"She attacked me," Haakan growled in protest. Wynflaed scowled back, her nice moment with Torben forgotten. The brute refused to see his behaviour, again treating her and her fellow captives like animals and not people.

"See, Guthred, she still tries to smite me!" he whined.

"Your men have no discipline," Torben observed, his eyes now on Guthred as his lips curled in disdain at the insolence.

"What do you care for a thrall, Torben?" asked Guthred, raising one eyebrow. "Ah, but I had forgotten you do not approve of slavery. Torben Hel-Bringer, killer of any who crossed his path, chose absolution by turning into a champion for the people."

Guthred's men laughed uncertainly, knowing their leader had made a joke but not understanding what it had meant.

"No, I do not care for humans being enslaved. You have seven what are they, Saxons? No doubt wrested violently from their homes, and for what? Coin? They are living, breathing humans, just like you and I."

Wynflaed heard the passion in his voice and silently cheered his words. However, Guthred remained unmoved.

Guthred shrugged. "It is the way of the world, old friend."

Every time Guthred said friend, he smothered it in a silky tone that dripped with bitterness. Wynflaed could taste it in her mouth. Though Torben's words had set her hopes to soar. Was he challenging Guthred with a goal to rescue her?

As she looked back at him, Wynflaed sensed Torben was losing patience as his eyes narrowed. That was all he allowed, as he was so controlled. He was skilled in making his point known in a disciplined way. His manner helped her feel anchored while her emotions spun out of control. Something about this drew her to him and piqued her curiosity. She heard Hilde groan as she tried to stand up and she quickly grabbed the woman to steady her, relieved she had found the strength to rise. Turning to Guthred, she intended to explain herself without any further hostility. Between that and Torben's intervention, she hoped he might see reason.

"My Lord, Guthred," she started, causing his men to laugh and his grin to widen. "Your man kicked poor Hilde after she had fallen. There was truly no cause for it."

"And what of you, little flower?" he said as he eyed her speculatively. "You shine brightly from your wash. Now, tell me what you did to cause such fury in Haakan."

She cringed at his scrutiny and him calling her a little flower as she tried her best for nonchalance.

"I was defending a friend." She was unable to stop the stubborn jut of her chin.

His men laughed again, as did he.

"I will need to sell you with a warning, I think. You come with a lot of fire," Guthred told her.

Wynflaed's stomach sank as the realisation of her situation struck again. She looked to Torben and she started when their eyes met. He was already staring at her. Pleading with her eyes, she silently begged him to do something. Why this stranger would help her she did not know, but she willed it with every fibre of her being.

"I will buy her," he spoke, turning back to Guthred. He said the word *buy* with distaste. What did he mean when he said *buy*? Buy her freedom or buy her life?

"What is this I hear? Torben the Hel-Bringer is to take a thrall?"

Torben did not reply, but his eyes narrowed dangerously at the insult. It gave her confidence he was buying her freedom.

Not knowing what might happen, she yelled, "And Hilde, too, please." She couldn't leave Hilde alone with these brutes.

Torben nodded, his eyes still on Guthred. As her saviour, Torben the Hel-Bringer, seemed agreeable, she made one last request. "And the remainder of my five companions. Please."

She felt the tension of the crowd as they all waited with bated breath for his response. Her plea for the freedom of herself and her fellow captives was entertainment to these people.

This time Torben's head did turn to her, his fair brows raised, but he smiled at her boldness. She blushed at this contact and the striking way the smile enhanced the beauty of his face. It was very unexpected, for before today, the last thing she could have imagined thinking was a Viking man having any beauty.

"I will take them all, Guthred. Ragnav will provide you with the coin."

Guthred had kept silent and now looked speculatively at Torben. Finally, he threw his hands up in the air.

"Sold. They are all yours. My *friend*."

This time, Wynflaed heard only a hard bitterness and a shiver ran up and down her spine. Guthred truly had a black soul. She glanced back at Haakan, who still stared at her with an evil glare, and she used all her willpower to not glare back. *Be the bigger person, Wynflaed*, she chanted in her head as she gestured for her fellow countrymen to follow her. But she was gleeful. And hopeful. She was also a little fretful as she saw Torben waiting for them in the dispersing crowd. Wynflaed heard a croak and looked upwards to the sky for the source. A black raven circled overhead and when she made eye contact, it held her gaze intently.

Was this an omen? Had she delivered them from one barbarian to another?

Chapter Four

Torben's cousin, Leif, was dumbstruck as he stood at the opening of one of their tents near the docks. His mouth hung open in horror as he looked at the ramshackle company Torben had returned with. Torben did not blame him for his shock at the sight of the pale, barefooted, half-starved beings that stood before them, shivering in their thin shifts. One glared furiously at Leif, the same one who had created the situation, noted Torben. Wynflaed, she had softly told him when he asked for her name. Torben found himself fascinated with her innocent ferocity. One moment cornered and afraid and a split second later hissing and in a rage. *Like a wild, trapped animal,* he thought, with no insult intended, for he found her a beautiful and intriguing woman.

Her amber eyes flashed, the colour deep and rich. He wanted to peer deeper into them and see what other flecks of colour he would find. He imagined strands of gold shot through those soulful irises. Her fair skin only enhanced their beauty, and he could picture a rosy glow to her cheeks if she was at her full health. Her unevenly shorn hair fell just above her shoulder. The raven curls bounced becomingly with every movement, as they highlighted her high cheekbones and full lips, reddened with cold. Her beauty stirred a passion he had not felt for a very long time, and he stiffened in his trousers. He pulled his cloak tighter around himself.

Get it together you fool! Look at all she has been through, he chastised himself and tried to focus on Leif's rant. He cursed his lack of self-control. He was better than this, he had never fallen powerless to his base desires.

"...we travel here to trade and gain wealth, not buy thralls to feed and clothe and do what? You do not allow thralls back home. What are they to do?"

Before Torben could answer Leif, who had been speaking in brokenly in her native tongue, not even trying to hide his frustration, the beauty, her eyes narrowed with dislike, interjected angrily.

"We can do many things. You should not judge us by our appearance at this moment. We were abducted from our homeland and treated poorly, like animals!"

Torben bit his lip to keep from laughing at Leif's shocked expression. His head turned from Wynflaed to Torben, mouth agape, no doubt at the audacity of this stranger's reprimand and Torben's acceptance of it.

Leif and his elder brother Sven were not only his cousins, but also his closest friends and advisors, and Torben gave them much responsibility in Klavik. He respected their right to speak their minds. Leif was closer to Torben's younger brother Ragnav in age, but while Ragnav was quick to joke and smile, Leif was serious with a witty sharp tongue. Whatever their differences, the two were so close people joked they had been born of the same womb. Leif's natural skill in trade had helped them prosper greatly over the years. Torben found it a fair exchange to deal with his tirades from time to time. As a bonus, they generally amused him.

"What has made Leif so upset? He looks like a fish out of

water with his mouth hanging open like that," Ragnav enquired with a wide grin as he returned from Torben's errand, waving his hand up and down in front of Leif's face.

"Leif has had the pleasure of meeting Wynflaed," Torben said with a smile and caught Wynflaed's eye. She blushed pink but held his stare in defiance. *Only a fool would try to dampen her fire,* he mused with a growing fondness he could see his younger brother shared.

"Ahh. Say no more," Ragnav choked out in between his guffaws.

"Did you find out any useful information?" Torben queried, as he gestured to Leif and Ragnav to step away with him.

"I did. There are two vessels sailing to the coast of Northumbria, a Danish trader and a pair of men from Irland. They all seem questionable, and I doubt they are men of their word," Ragnav informed them. His younger brother had good instincts. If he doubted their honour, they were not good men.

It was better that they accompany him home, but he wanted them to have free will. He needed to explain the options and their risks and allow them to choose, or he would be no better than Guthred. He could not help but hope that Wynflaed would choose to stay with him. He sensed her path was tied with his, he just needed time to explore it at his own pace. But he did not want to influence her free will, as that went against what he believed in. Her spirit intrigued him, and she was a contradiction in all ways. She was hard and soft. Innocent and worldly. Stalling would prove to be no reprieve, so Torben summoned his resolve and walked over to Wynflaed and the others. He took in their wide-eyed gazes. They were cold and hungry, and he needed to remedy that. Their wellbeing was now his responsibility.

"It is clear to all that you have suffered greatly. I am a man of my word. I do not keep thralls in my home or on my lands. Everyone earns their keep but the choice whether to cook, fight, mend, or heal is theirs. I bought you your freedom and I will not take this choice away from you now."

He paused as his eyes locked with Wynflaed's. She watched him intently as she took in every word. Holding her gaze, he continued.

"You have three options. No matter which option you choose, I will give you clothing, food, and some coin," he said, ignoring Leif's groan of protest. "You can stay here in Kyivan Rus and start a new life. I only pass through these lands for trade and know few details of them to share with you. Your second choice is one of two ships travelling to Northumbria. I do not know these captains and I cannot guarantee your safety. Your third option is to return with me to Klavik, where I am Chieftain and start anew as free people."

His gaze travelled across the group as he spoke, but when he explained the last option, his eyes found Wynflaed's again and he searched them for a reaction when he mentioned Klavik. Her face was inscrutable. All he saw was her brow furrowed in concentration as she considered her choices. A nervous weight settled in the pit of his stomach as he waited for her answer. He wanted to unravel who Wynflaed was down to her core. What made her smile, what made her weep. Never had a woman intrigued him this way. He heard the croak of a raven and looked up to see one perched on a wooden post by the dock. It was a sign that he was right in feeling this way. And Odin approved. But would Wynflaed? He wished he could have a small glimpse into her mind and all the beautiful chaos he pictured there.

Stay with me, Wynflaed.

Chapter Five

Wynflaed felt like she was back home in Northumbria, standing at the edge of one of the craggy cliffs that rose above the rough seas. She had gotten too close when she was little and remembered the terrifying feeling one misstep would send her falling over the edge into the crashing waves. That sound echoed in her head as she considered her choice. One step would decide whether she prospered or went to her demise. Her future was on the precipice, this decision would shape her life.

She knew she did not want to stay here, in this Kyivan Rus. And while she yearned for the comfort and security of her life back in Northumbria, something drew her to Torben. Her saviour. Never had a man looked at her with such intensity. It was not the simple lust of the boys she knew at home. It was something more, something hungry. She struggled to find a word to aptly describe the heat that spread through her body. And the worst thing about the feeling was it excited her more than it scared her. Since her capture, she had blossomed from meek and mild to rash and tempestuous.

Was this who I always was? Who I am? Can I trust myself to make this choice? She turned to Hilde for wisdom.

"Hilde, what shall we do?"

"I will go wherever you choose. I am indebted to you," the older woman said in assurance. But this did not help Wynflaed decide. It only increased the burden that loomed over her.

"We have repaid each other, Hilde. You protected me, and I protected you," Wynflaed gently reminded her. Hilde gave her a nod of understanding but still offered no opinion. Trust shone in her kind brown eyes as she placed her life in Wynflaed's hands.

"How many summers have you seen, Hilde?" she asked.

"Thirty-seven, child."

Wynflaed had recently passed her twenty-second. *By common standards, they were both old maids. What kind of life did they have waiting for them back in Northumbria? But what would they do in Klavik?*

She looked back at Torben who still watched her as Leif spoke to him with gesturing hands. Leif clearly thought this was a bad idea and she could not blame him. They were strangers in every way.

A ray of sunlight poked through the grey clouds and caught Torben's fair hair, highlighting his rugged handsomeness. She spied a faint scar through one of his brows and another on his cheek. The sides of his head were shaved, and the rest of his hair was long—longer than her own now— and pulled into a tight plait at the back of his head. She lifted her hand to her tresses, feeling the short uneven length. While she knew it looked unsightly, the missing hair gave her a lightness. She had never realised hair would hold a noticeable weight. Hilde, who was watching her, gave her a look of guilt. Mistaking Wynflaed's musings for distress, she wrung her hands.

"I am sorry about your hair, Wynflaed. I only sought to

protect you when I cut it. You are very fair, and I had hoped cutting your hair and the smell of fish and dirt would disguise your beauty and keep them from looking at you too closely. Men are drawn to your beauty and some men, like those who captured us, will seek you out against your will."

Wynflaed nodded, the gravity of their current circumstances not lost on her when Hilde spoke of savage lust-filled men. And there was no man here she trusted save for Torben, even though he was still a stranger. He had already proven his kindness in rescuing them. That action showed her he was a good man. Her decision would have to be based on faith and instinct. She had ruled out Kyivan Rus, which left her the choice of risking a ship back home or travelling to a new land with a stranger.

Cola caught her attention, his sister Cynewin close at his side. They were siblings, both younger than she. Cola had dark features that belied the meaning of his name. Cynewin was a wisp of a girl with mousy hair and huge brown eyes who had barely spoken a word and clung to her brother's side. The others were all men of different ages who had been intent on looking out for themselves. Wynflaed did not judge them but did not hold feelings for them either. The siblings, though, were sweet and they now looked to her for advice.

"Wynflaed, what are you to do?" he said. "The others are going to return on a ship back to Northumbria. I do not think that is wise for my sister and me, but I do not wish us to stay here either." His dark brown eyes flashed with indecision and a plea for guidance.

Wynflaed took a deep breath and closed her eyes. She pictured the sky, the ocean, the green earth. She pictured freedom. A freedom not guaranteed if they returned home to Northumbria. Their path was clear. She would decide the fate of them all and face the consequences, come what may.

"Hilde, Cola, and Cynewin, we will go with Chieftain

Torben back to his home in Klavik. Of all our choices, this seems the safest option where we may survive and have a chance to live out our lives."

All three of them nodded. They still looked a little nervous but also relieved a decision had been made. Wynflaed watched Torben head over to the three men. He nodded and pointed them towards Leif, his expression resigned, but holding bundles of clothing. Torben turned and their eyes locked again. Her pulse quickened as he approached them with the intensity of a wolf circling its prey. Instead of making her feel frightened, she was excited. The flutter in her heart was like a butterfly in flight, and it signalled the stir of passion deep inside her.

"Wynflaed, what choice do you make?"

Chapter Six

Torben wished the three men well and followed through with his offer to clothe, feed, and provide them with some coin. Despite Leif's grumbling over the cost, it was no real concern. Their own wealth was plenty, their trade successful, and their lands had prospered well in their last harvest. He did not dismiss Leif's concerns lightly, he had a shrewd mind for business, but being humane would always come first. And despite his grumbling, Torben knew Leif was less disapproving of the gesture than he seemed. His cousin did have a kind and giving heart.

Wynflaed stood slightly in front of the remaining freed captives, who huddled together and showed their deference to her as their voice. She stood tall as he approached, flashing a bold, amber-eyed gaze that spoke of decision. A Northumbrian Wynflaed may be, but she had the strength and spirit of a Valkyrie. As was her beauty. He stopped a short distance before the group and offered a small smile to the youngest woman who trembled in what he hoped was not fear.

"Wynflaed, what choice do you make?" He hated the fretfulness being displayed in his voice for all to hear.

"We shall go with you, my lord," she said. She followed this up with an awkward curtsy as did Hilde, while the young man gave a bow. Torben was confused by the sudden formality. He did not like a meek and mild Wynflaed.

He had no reasonable right to feel the relief that spread from his fingers to his toes when she gave him her answer. He had not wanted to sway her free will before their decision, but now he opened his arms wide in invitation to share more of his life.

"I am very pleased to hear this. And yes, I am what you would call a Lord, I am Chieftain to my people. I have laws but I am fair. As I said, we have no thralls, everyone chooses what they will do with their life and is compensated. We live mostly in peace but will battle anyone who comes to do us harm. My land is in Norway, a place called Klavik. It is a bay settlement where my ancestors have lived for centuries."

"Do we need to decide now what work we will do?" Wynflaed asked, and he shook his head.

"There is time for you to consider this, we have the journey back and you will need to see our lands. I assume you all have a skill of some kind?" They all nodded except for Wynflaed who blushed at the comment. Strange. Not wanting to cause any embarrassment, he changed the subject.

"Let us find you clothing and food. We will need to go to a trader who caters to women, as I am afraid that what we have will all be too big. But first, what are everyone's names?" He looked first to the young man. *He is scrawny, but he has a large frame he will likely grow into*, Torben thought with approval.

"My name is Cola, milord, and this is my sister Cynewin. I am grateful to you for saving us. We already know what we can offer. I am a skilled hunter and butcher and Cynewin here is a fine weaver."

"Those skills are always most welcome, thank you Cola and Cynewin. Cola, go grab your clothes and footwear from Leif and we will set off," he said, knowing the siblings would not want to be separated for too long. Their youth made them even more vulnerable then Wynflaed and Hilde. He was relieved they had also decided to come with him.

"And of course, I know your name is Hilde." He spoke in a kind tone to the older woman Wynflaed had defended. Her hair was a shade of grey, but her face remained unlined. Only when she smiled did her skin crinkle at the corners.

"It is, indeed, and I am also grateful for all you have done for us. I can be of use as a minder of children, as a washerwoman or as a weaver."

"A person with many skills is always welcome, Hilde." He could see this compliment pleased her as she beamed a smile. Of the group, she seemed the most at ease in his presence.

"And I know you are Wynflaed, but Cola is returning so we can discuss your skills at a different time."

Torben saw the relief wash over her face.

Why was she embarrassed by this subject? What profession had she had? Was she a whore of some kind back in her homeland?

The thought of other men touching her caused a wave of jealousy. Searching her soft profile, he decided against it, she looked too innocent.

They found a trader from the East who sold women's wear. Their goods occupied many rows of tents and stalls and included clothing, fabric, and shoes for men, women, and children. It was still light of day when the chill in the air eased slightly as more sunlight shone through the clouds. The shop owner gestured the women to a tent they could use to change. Torben stood directly outside, feeling obligated to protect their modesty.

Torben outfitted each with a pair of sturdy leather boots,

thick woollen stockings, and dresses to go over the linen shifts they wore. The ill-fitting shifts hung loose, giving the women no shape and he wondered what Wynflaed hid under the garment. They would be provided with proper clothing tailored to their bodies when they returned home. Last, he gave them heavy cloaks. The cloaks and his pelts would ensure they kept warm on their voyage home. It was clear they were not seafaring people and their journey thus far had been an unpleasant experience.

The seas were cold at night, and they could not light fires on the ships for warmth. The group, now clothed and warm, looked considerably happier and it made his heart glow with the satisfaction of helping them. *If only the idea of Wynflaed was not warming my loins, it would be a selfless act*, he thought ruefully, as it was her that his mind kept coming back to. He watched her smiling face as she pulled the cloak tight and sank into its warmth. It was a drastic change from how he had found her, fighting for her life. She revelled in her freedom, and it was glorious to witness. He would never understand the slave trade, the way humans dehumanised other humans. Freeing these people was fate and, in a way, his own atonement for the part he had played in the bloodshed of their people. *When I return to Klavik, I will make a sacrifice to Odin for honouring my path.*

Chapter Seven

Wynflaed inhaled the scented steam of the piping hot stew before her. After Torben had clothed them, he steered them to a busier area where she could smell the aromas of both familiar and unfamiliar foods. He found them a table and chairs and, within moments, food appeared. The wooden bowl warmed her hands. The stew smelt of lamb and carrots and potatoes but with tantalising spices, unlike the pottage she was accustomed to back home. Lifting the bowl to her mouth, she unwittingly let out a sigh of pleasure and caught Torben watching her. From the half smile and twinkle in his blue eyes, she knew he had heard her sigh.

"I have not eaten this well for some time," she reminded him, knowing it came out more defensively than she intended, but he continued to smile. For whatever reason, he seemed to find her annoyance and curt behaviour charming.

"Enjoy your meals, all of you, and seconds and thirds if necessary. No doubt you all need to rebuild your strength."

He was so very kind. And as irrational as it seemed, she felt annoyed by it. The sight of him was pleasurable to the eyes, but his kindness was contrary to all the stories she had heard of Vikings.

"How do you come to speak our tongue so well, Chieftain Torben?" At her question, she thought she saw a slight shadow pass over his face.

"Please, just Torben. I spent much time in your land, learning the native tongue. Trading from land to land across the oceans has also allowed me to pick up many different languages. Much of my settlement can speak, or at least somewhat understand, as we once had Mercians live among us."

"If I may be so bold, may I ask another question?"

He nodded with a smile at her polite request, and she bit her cheek knowing her behaviour in the short time she had known him had been anything but polite.

"You may, Wynflaed."

"Why did that man Guthred keep calling you his friend?"

His face hardened and she worried she had misspoken. It was obvious there was a dark history between him and Guthred.

"While you may ask the question, the answer will be for another day." His tone was hard, matching his expression.

She nodded and turned her attention back to her food. This was her first glimpse of his other side. He was a man, after all, and Viking, but intrinsically she knew that he could keep that side of himself in check. Wynflaed knew it would not be prudent to push and she was placated that he would share the story with her one day. A hunk of fresh brown bread had been provided with the meal and she tore off chunks to sop up the remaining stew in the bowl.

More questions raced through her mind but she kept silent, not wanting to push her luck. He seemed a tolerant man, especially for one of his rank as a Viking. She did not want to press and see more of the other side that lurked underneath. Somehow, she doubted she would, but, after what she had endured, she had learned to be on her guard.

Wynflaed found no further opportunity to examine Torben's personality and she had to admit she was disappointed. Within days, he had finished his trading and Ragnav led them to the two great Viking ships they were to sail to Klavik upon, much larger and more impressive than the one they had arrived on with Guthred. At the keels of the longships were intricately carved figureheads of ravens, two of them joined as one, facing in opposite directions. They were so detailed she could imagine the realistic carvings detaching themselves from the ship and flying away. The carved eyes seemed to follow her gaze. It unnerved her as much as it was impossible to look away from. A giant raven that would terrify both those at sea and on land. Ragnav must have seen her staring at them, and he gestured to the figureheads proudly.

"The ravens are Odin's symbol. And these ravens are to honour Huginn and Muninn, the ravens that sit on Odin's shoulders. They are his eyes and ears and bring him information from the world, from Midgard. Having their presence on our ship ensures our safe passage, as their knowledge helps us navigate the seas home."

The storytelling fascinated her, and he spoke her language as well as Torben. Being born a Christian, she knew it was unholy to be so intrigued, but this story about one of their gods touched her in a way the story of the Holy Saviour never had. Wynflaed shook her head free of religious thoughts.

Though she was not overjoyed to be at sea once again, this journey was more comfortable, at least. She barely saw Torben, just glimpses of him managing his crew. Ragnav, a charmer if there ever was one, tended to all their needs. He was jovial and always smiling, like the pups she remembered playing with back home.

Before they left, Ragnav had explained that a longship was built for speed and harsh weather conditions. It had an undercover area that stored the goods, keeping them dry. As this space was mainly empty on the return home, it was a good place for the women to keep warm and comfortable. The space, while not overly large, was still comfortable for all three of the women to sit. Cola chose to sit with the men rowing and help when he could, not having the strength to pull the oars himself for too long.

still comfortable for all three of the women to sit. Cola had chosen to sit with the men rowing and help where he could, not having the strength to pull the oars himself for too long, but he wanted to help where he could.

Ragnav had kindly sourced a chamber pot, a wash bowl, and a comb for each of the women and gave the items to them with a handsome bow. The combs were made of deer antler and the handles were inlaid with silver. They came in their own wooden boxes etched with flowers that had been prettily coloured with pigments of blue and yellow. He had explained that it was important to have your own comb and care for your hair which was a symbol of pride. Wynflaed was touched by his thoughtfulness. They were Norse-made, as he had been careful to buy them from another Northern trader, for Ragnav boasted no one took care of their hair better than his people. His own hair was, indeed, well cared for, it shone brightly and was intricately plaited.

Wynflaed felt grateful for his attentions. The women passed their time with stories and sleep, and the arrival of Ragnav and Cole with food and the emptying of their chamber pot was a welcome interruption to the monotony.

Ragnav generally shared a tale or two. Her favourite stories he had shared so far were about Odin's Valkyries, his battle maidens. The imagery of their silky golden hair and startling white skin was so vivid, she easily pictured the silver-armoured women and their snow-white steeds. The story of Brunhild, the daughter of Odin who defied him, was her favourite. It amazed and inspired her that a woman, even a brave shield-maiden, would challenge the wrath of her gods. She found it even more romantic that Sigurd, a mortal man, would face the ring of fire that Odin had cursed to surround her while she slept everlasting. Her appreciation of the tale made Ragnav laugh, and he told her she reminded him a little of Brunhild herself. These stories and learning more of the way of the Norse helped time pass quickly.

She learned more about Hilde and tried to bring Cynewin out of her shell. None of them had ever left Northumbria prior to their abduction, and they had all been born lower class. Hilde had tidied up the uneven length of Wynflaed's hair, which now fell more nicely. Once a day, they stepped out onto the deck of the ship for air and light, but Torben kept a distance. She thought it was on purpose and she hoped he could feel the cross look she sent his way. She had counted more than a *seofon nihta* before she heard the deep blowing of a horn and a cheer from the men. It appeared they would soon arrive in Klavik.

Chapter Eight

Torben stood by the raven figurehead, giving his thanks to the gods for another voyage that had brought them safely home. He rubbed the carved oak and breathed in the sharp, clean air that only the mountain-surrounded bay could create. One of his men sounded the horn, two short blasts and one long note to let their people know they would soon arrive. This familiar ritual always filled him with calm.

Ragnav came to stand by his side, inhaling sharply as well.

"Nothing smells quite like home, does it, brother?" He sighed contentedly next to Torben.

"Any absence makes me all the more grateful when I see it," he replied with a nod.

"I could never leave here. Why do the Norse want to live anywhere but here?" Ragnav said with a shake of his head. "Our people are going to be surprised by the four we've brought home."

"Yes, but they will adjust. We have good-hearted people. Tell me brother, how does Wyn—how do the women fare?" Torben cursed inwardly at his slip of the tongue. Ragnav seemed not to notice and spoke on.

"They are well, but eager to land. I have been regaling them with tales. Wynflaed has taken to stories of the Valkyrie, especially the tale of Brunhild."

Torben smiled, unsurprised that the fiery beauty's interests aligned with those of the shield-maidens.

"She would make a fine shield-maiden, don't you think, Ragnav?"

"With all that courage she would, she is a fierce one," Ragnav agreed enthusiastically. "That Wynflaed, she is also a beauty. The men will be eager to meet her. I think I shall make a claim on her."

Torben spun to face his brother.

"No, you will not!" he said furiously, feeling the blood rush to the surface of his body. It receded just as quickly when he saw the twinkling mirth in his brother's eye. Torben sighed. He had been baited and fallen for it like a fool.

"Come now, Torben, you are enthralled by her. Why do you never allow yourself any pleasure?"

"Being Chieftain gives me little time for pleasure and, in any case, after you are done enjoying all the pleasures in life, there is little left for me."

Ragnav laughed, enjoying their exchange.

"Was that a jest you made, Torben, or do you give insult to my lack of responsibility? Whichever way, I welcome you stepping outside your serious self."

"I think it was a little of both. I can admit I do envy you, Ragnav, just a small bit. But then I hear of your latest lover's quarrel and I am glad to not be you."

"You will never see me sorry for my ability to please women well enough they will fight for another chance to lie with me," he replied with a wink.

Torben was unable to hold back a smile. He truly loved his brother's passion for life. It would never be his path to be so carefree. Ragnav was a strong and able warrior, but he had never wet his sword or swung his axe in the same battles Torben had. *Torben Hel-Bringer, that is who I am.* He would never shed that moniker.

He heard female voices and turned to see the women had come on deck to watch the sights as they drew closer to Klavik. The mountains rose high on each side of the bay and the water became calmer and clearer, the shades of blue swirling invitingly. Torben watched Wynflaed's face alight with wonder as she took in the top of the mountains, snowcapped and sparkling where a waterfall flowed. The beauty she saw in his home was the same beauty he saw in her, radiant and unadulterated. He felt a pull on the thread that seemed to tie her to him. He missed the sound of her husky voice and her sharp wit. Unable to keep his distance, he called out to her.

"Wynflaed, come to where I stand and see Klavik as we approach."

She raised a mocking eyebrow and he knew she had noticed his distance on the voyage. But it had done nothing to assuage his interest while he brooded over her. He crooked his finger at her and a smile spread across his face.

She came over slowly but surely, holding his gaze till she stood beside him, her posture defensive.

"I wondered if you would ever speak to me again, *my lord.*"

He felt satisfied that his distance had raised her ire.

"I have been busy navigating my ship, Wynflaed, but it warms me to know it bothered you so."

This brought a blush to her face, and he savoured the sight.

"I am not bothered by it at all, *Torben.*"

He threw back his head and laughed at her tone. In the corner of his eye, he saw the men closest to him lift their heads in surprise at hearing him laugh this way. They were close enough to Klavik now to hear his people cheering at their return and he swept his arm across the front of his body.

"What do you think of Klavik so far?"

"It is very beautiful. It almost does not seem real." Any ire in her tone had vanished and he could only hear awe at the imagery before them. Having been to Northumbria, he tried to see it through her fresh eyes. He knew these sights differed vastly from her homeland.

"We have many long houses, many trade fronts. I am very proud of what my people have built over years of hard labour." She nodded. They were close enough to see the edge of the town that lay beyond the piers where the ships docked.

"Have you thought any more about what you might do here?" he asked her.

"I have been thinking, though I am still unsure."

Her posture was tense again, her voice guarded.

"Do not worry, Wynflaed. I think I know what you can do here."

Chapter Nine

He wants me to do what? she screamed inside as she tried to wrap her mind around his proposition.

"...you will like my sister. She has lost some of her spirit and needs help running the household."

Sister? Household? He had not been speaking of making me his concubine but a handmaiden to his sister and steward of his home!

Wynflaed had never felt so flooded with different emotions all at once. His gaze had been heated when he spoke those words, drenched with carnal desire. She felt excitement and lust burgeoning deep inside her, but also anger at the thought that he would treat her so. His blue eyes and plaited fair hair contrasted so beautifully against his sun-tanned skin and she envisioned what his strong body would be like underneath his clothing.

She blushed so strongly at her wanton and ambitious presumption that he had wanted her in his bed that she felt like she had stuck her face in a roaring fire. He stared at her quizzically as she opened and closed her mouth, unable to think of any appropriate response. Luckily she was saved from having to say anything as they had pulled up too close to the din and were getting ready to depart the ship. The men brought up the oars as they manoeuvred the longship to dock.

She cast a sideways glance at him, pondering what he had said. His chiselled profile was a thing of beauty, how could she not want this man? In truth, she had been avoiding the topic of what skills she could bring to the settlement as she was a simple handmaiden. She had never imagined he would give her such an important task. The more she considered it, the more she realised she was capable of supporting his sister. Her handmaiden skills would aid her. And running a settlement? She had already spent the last few years observing these duties. Surely, she could put them to use.

Wynflaed saw the people of Klavik eyeing her curiously, likely identifying her as a foreigner. Many in the crowd were tall, fair-haired, and smiling. All the tales about their heathenism had made her envision unclean people, but everyone she cast her gaze on looked well-kept. Much better than the serfs back home, who rarely washed. There was the smell of fresh fish and wood smoke, an earthy aroma and not unpleasant. She kept close behind Torben, Ragnav behind her with Hilde and Cynewin as they moved through the crowd. There was so much chatter and laughter, it was overwhelming. She hoped Cynewin and Cola were doing well and she tried to see them around Ragnav's large frame.

"To the hall for mead and tales!" Torben's booming voice rang out to more resounding cheers, and the crowd thinned. They made their way to a longhouse and its sheer size was impressive. The wooden structure was long–like its name–and tall, covered with intricate carvings she noted as they got close enough for her to see. The opening arch had carved wooden ravens that beckoned them inside and Torben ushered them to the dais.

"My good people of Klavik, how good it is to be home and

see your faces full of health and joy. As you can see, I have brought newcomers that will settle with us. Their stories are their own. I will share with you briefly that they were taken forcibly from their homes, and I have promised them safe and protected lives here in Klavik. It goes without saying that you will welcome them and help them settle in."

Wynflaed watched as his people cheered and lifted their flagons. He spoke Norse but translated his words for Wynflaed, Hilde, Cynewin, and Cola. As she scanned the crowd, she saw mainly composed faces, unperturbed by their arrival. It made the few that looked suspicious stand out more. She locked eyes with a handsome woman who watched her with a narrowed gaze. Wynflaed broke the stare, but she was left with an uncomfortable feeling in the pit of her stomach. Torben spoke with an animated Hilde and she stepped closer to his side to join their conversation.

"Ah, thank you, Hilde. Your skills are well welcomed, but before you get started, please eat, wash, and sleep. It has been a long journey for you all. I will have you, Cynewin, and Wynflaed escorted to our bathhouses," he told her warmly, evidently charmed by her spirit.

"I would like to meet your sister first, Torben, if I may?" Wynflaed asked him.

Torben nodded as he looked at her contemplatively. The intensity of his gaze made her squirm a little and she tried to keep still, not wanting him to know he was unnerving her. She wanted to see what she was to expect from his sister. She found it curious she had not come to welcome them.

"Olga, can you please show Hilde and Cynewin to the bathhouses? Get Cola on the way, I can see him talking with Ragnav."

The big-boned woman came forward with a welcoming smile. She used her hands to gesture to them as she said "Come, come," in her heavy accent.

"Olga is one of the many blessings to our people. She is too set in her ways to learn languages, but finds her ways to communicate." Torben's blue eyes were still fixed upon her face.

"She seems wonderful, a kind spirit shines around her." She nodded, sensing Olga's goodness.

Wynflaed noticed his posture had become tense, and he seemed to be choosing his words carefully. She waited patiently for him to speak, wanting him to know he could trust her.

"Before I take you to meet my sister, I will share something with you." He paused and scanned her face as if he was searching for something. Understanding? Approval?

"Yes, please share it with me," she urged, sensing the concern in his voice, and she touched her hand to his wrist as a sign of assurance. She felt a tingle at the skin to skin contact but she did not move her hand. She saw he had felt it as well, his face a mix of heat and curiosity at the spark of physical attraction. But the moment passed quickly as his mind turned back to his sister. She saw the physical change in him, something about her weighed heavily on him.

"My sister, Freydis, suffered an incident some years ago and that has left her face scarred. She is withdrawn at times and suffers deep bouts of sadness that worsen as she gets older. You have a fiery spirit, Wynflaed. I think you can help her see her worth beyond what is skin deep."

Wynflaed's heart clenched at the pain and sadness she heard in his voice. Torben cared deeply for his sister.

"I would love to help Freydis, Torben, take me to her."

Torben led her to the back of the longhouse into a small room that had a fire burning. The room was bare except for a table and chair, where a woman sat.

"Freydis" Torben spoke softly, "I am home, and I have brought someone I would like you to meet."

Wynflaed wondered if he had spoken too softly as the fair-headed figure did not move. Her hair was like spun silk, plaited with intricate detail in ropes that fell down her back. Just when she thought Torben would speak again, she started to turn and Wynflaed came face to face with the most beautiful girl she had ever seen. Her eyes differed from Torben's, more green than blue, and her features were ethereal in their femininity. She almost did not seem real. But along the left side of her cheek was a jagged, puckered scar that ran from the corner of her eye to the tip of her chin. It was a pale red in colour, not yet healed white, and Wynflaed's heart went out to the girl at the pain that wound must have caused her.

"Ugly, isn't it?" she said in a melodious but hardened tone as she stared defiantly at Torben before casting her gaze on Wynflaed.

She knew the response she made now would determine whether she and Freydis would be friends or foes. Wynflaed searched her feelings and realised she felt no pity. She felt empathy that such a tragedy had occurred, but pity? Feeling sorry for Freydis would not help her. Forthright honesty would.

Chapter Ten

Torben observed his sister and Wynflaed as they took stock of each other. Freydis, his beautiful and once carefree sister, had hardened a tough outer shell he could not crack. Worst of all, most of the blame lay with him. She blamed him for not letting her choose a path she believed would lead to her happiness. Wynflaed, to her credit, had neither flinched nor shown any surprise at the scar or cold welcome. She simply returned Freydis's greeting with a warm smile.

"I am pleased to meet you, Freydis. And no, I do not think it is ugly. It may not be sightly, but a scar is usually a sign of bravery or overcoming something that could have been more dire. And even with the scar, Freydis, you are truly the most beautiful girl I have ever seen."

Freydis snorted in derision.

"I was. I can admit that vanity. Perhaps that is why the gods thought to punish me and take away my beauty."

"I disagree, Freydis. God, or your gods, gives hardships to the strong, knowing they can overcome them. But it is clear I will need time to help you see what I see." Wynflaed spoke plainly and firmly, brooking no argument.

"Why are you here?" Freydis asked, curiosity now entering her hard tone.

Torben was glad his instincts in pairing these two had been right. Wynflaed had handled the meeting exactly as he had hoped. Without any hubris, just honest words with no pity. And he knew his sister well enough to know Wynflaed had engaged her interest once he saw her posture relax.

"It would be best for Torben to explain, he only briefly shared his intentions when we arrived onshore," Wynflaed told her, giving him a disgruntled look.

Torben's brow lifted in surprise at her reaction, but he brushed it aside and answered the question.

"Wynflaed and three more of her people have come to make homes with us here in Klavik. If it pleases her, Wynflaed will assist you in taking care of things around here and be of company to you. I sense a kindred spirit and hope you two bring each other joy."

Wynflaed nodded her approval and Freydis gave the slightest of nods as she continued to stare at Wynflaed with curiosity.

"I would very much like that, Freydis. I was a handmaiden back in Northumbria and have knowledge of how a manor or, in this instance, a settlement is run. I like the idea of putting things in order and I will need you to help me learn the ways of your people."

Freydis shrugged. "I never cared for this role, and it is not like I shall ever marry." She threw a hard pointed look at Torben. "So why not? Let us do it together."

Torben sighed at Freydis's petulance and gave a sad shake of his head.

"I think only of your safety and happiness, Freydis."
Will she ever forgive me?
He turned to Wynflaed, who watched their exchange. No doubt she would have questions he was not prepared to

answer. He clapped his hands loudly in an attempt to break the solemn mood.

"Come, Wynflaed. I will take you to the bathhouses."

Torben was silent as he escorted Wynflaed to the bathhouses. It was still daylight, and he could see every emotion that flickered across her face. He knew that she had many questions for him and was surprised she held her tongue. As they approached the bathhouse, he saw her take in the sights of the settlement with wonderment and his excitement to show them to her grew. Differently sized huts, designed to fit single or multiple people, were positioned in a circle with a well in the middle. Bathing was often a social time for the men and the women.

"This is our bathing area," he said, with a proud wave of his hand, "which is constructed atop natural hot water springs."

He saw Wynflaed's eyes light with pleasure at the idea of hot water.

"How wonderful, Torben," she said, sighing with want.

"There is a stream through those trees but the structures are either bath or steam houses. If you want to bathe, go into a bathhouse where the water is kept warm by the enclosed building. The steam houses are filled with rocks that create a mist you can sit in and then you can go cool off in the stream."

"Why are they all different sizes?" she asked, pointing to the huts.

"Some are for small groups, some women only, some men only and one room is filled with cloths and soaps. Here. I will go grab some if you want to go into that hut there." He nudged her toward one of the smaller buildings.

He grabbed a bar of floral soap brought by a trader and a drying cloth. He entered the hut and saw she had already stripped to her shift. A pounding began to beat in his veins as his arousal grew.

"Ahh...Wynflaed, here you go." He felt awkward as he handed her the soap and cloth.

"Thank you," she said shyly as she grabbed the items, but he did not let go. His self-control was beginning to wane. In order to change the subject and shift the tension in the air away from the crackling heat between them, he decided to raise her temper instead.

"What caused you to be so offended with me earlier, Wynflaed? He saw a pink tinge spread from her face and chest to her arms and legs.

"I thought you were going to propose an improper task to me," she told him in a slightly huskier tone and stepped closer to pull the items from his grip. He let them go but took a step forward as well. This was the last response he had expected from her.

"But I did not, so why do you still appear bothered by it, Wynflaed?" She was close enough now that he could see the arousal reflected in her amber gaze. He had not raised her temper but instead raised her lust, which was now burgeoning with his own.

She did not answer, just moistened her lips and he helplessly watched her tongue lave the plump pout. The slip of her little tongue was innocent but enticing and he groaned. His fiery little Wynflaed was not averse to him, but she was still an innocent maiden in a foreign land.

He did not want to take advantage of her, but every fibre of his being told him to capture those sweet, full lips with his own. He cupped her head and spread his fingers through her soft raven curls to pull her closer to his lips. She did not pull away but parted her lips in invitation, which he accepted with a soft growl as a primal urge took over.

He covered her mouth with his own and drank in her passion as she threw her arms around his neck and pressed her soft body to his. His tongue swept her mouth and she met it with her own, fiery and sweetly erotic as her inexperience fuelled her exploration. He pulled her tightly against his body, one hand still at the nape of her neck and the other at the small of her back. He throbbed against her as he imagined the soft wetness between her legs and kissed her hungrily. A voice of sanity reminded him that he was not a man to take someone's innocence, and he forced himself to let her go. He looked down at her ravished face and swollen lips as she breathed heavily.

"I am sorry, Wynflaed. I lost myself, my control. Forgive me. Take your bath and I will have Olga wait for you." He reluctantly let her go and walked abruptly out of the hut. He sensed her confusion and anger, but he did not turn back. He could not trust himself. In the face of her obvious want and the throbbing ache between his legs, he was close to throwing any good sense aside and taking her then and there.

In the name of all the gods, what have I done?

Chapter Eleven

Wynflaed settled into the soothing warm water of the hot spring and swore an oath at her wanton behaviour. No doubt, Torben thought she was immoral. *Maybe that is why he pulled away.* Sniffing the cake of soap, she inhaled the scents of lavender, lemon balm and other florals she had yet to discover. She scrubbed her skin furiously with the soap before moving on to her tresses, massaging her scalp in an attempt to relieve the tension.

After she had scrubbed herself from head to toe, she grabbed a wooden bucket that sat on the edge of the bath and used it to pour water over her hair and body. She stood up, the water level just below her waist and enjoyed the water sluicing down her body. She repeated the action a few times before she set the bucket down and travelled her hands down her body. She felt the smooth curves of her breasts, then moved down to her waist and the small of her back before she spread her hands out across her buttocks.

She blushed as she remembered the heat that had emanated from between her legs at Torben's kisses and moved her hand to the curls that covered the area, unable to refrain from touching herself there. She knew it was unholy but in this moment she did not care. She was not a virgin but had little experience. She had only experienced the carnal knowledge of a man a handful of times and had found little joy in it. But the desire that Torben had wrought in her body was so delectable she wanted to know the feeling again and again, so she rubbed herself harder and faster, fascinated by the sensations spreading through her extremities.

She had not been aware her body could feel this way as she tensed and her breath started to come out in pants. All of a sudden something deep inside her exploded and she felt a wetness between her legs that was not from the water. She felt more free, more alive, and more satisfied than she ever had before. She sat back down in the bath to catch her breath and felt both slightly proud and slightly ashamed of the pleasure. She could not help but imagine how much more pleasure she could feel if Torben touched her, was inside of her.

She heard a tap at the door and Olga's voice.

"I am here when you ready, Wynflaed. I have clean clothes for you," she said.

"Yes, Olga, I just need to dry myself."

Wynflaed quickly used the cloth to dry her skin and then wrapped the material around herself before she opened the door and poked her head out. Olga handed her a clean linen shift, a moss-green dress with long sleeves, and woollen hose for her feet.

"It gets much cold at night," Olga told her with a smile.

Wynflaed returned her smile with thanks, closed the door, and quickly dressed herself. The clothes all fit a little loosely, but Olga had clearly taken the hem up in consideration of her shorter stature. The dress flattered her figure nicely after she tightened the strings around the bodice. A floral motif was stitched over the bust in a brown thread, and she fingered the pretty pattern. She pulled on the hose as high as they could go and then slipped on the leather shoes Torben had bought her. Lastly, she placed the cloak around her shoulders, another reminder of Torben. She gave it a sniff. It was due for a wash, but she would leave that for another time. She bundled up the rest of the clothing and stepped out to meet Olga.

"You have nice hair," Olga said with admiration as her wet curls slowly dried and sprang back into shape while they walked through the crisp air back towards the hubbub of the settlement.

"Thank you, Olga. I will need to comb it out before it gets too unruly," she said, laughing.

"I take you to room. Torben give you room next to Freydis in the main house."

She could only assume this meant she would be sleeping in the same quarters as Torben. A shiver of anticipation ran down her spine.

"What of Hilde, Cynewin, and Cola?" she queried, realising she had not seen her comrades in some time now.

"Cynewin and Cola have been given hut and Hilde sleep in the women's longhouse. Olga there, Olga take care of her," Olga said with a reassuring nod.

Olga led her into a large longhouse that held colourful tapestries, ancient wooden carvings inlaid with precious metals, and luxurious pelts that spoke to the nobility of the Ulfsons. Men and women sat on wooden benches on either side of a long fire pit, perhaps waiting to speak with Torben, as they looked to see who had come through the door. The people smiled at her when she passed and she smiled back, relieved that no one here gave her any looks of animosity.

Olga led her through heavy fur curtains to a hallway with several doors. She pointed at each room.

"Chieftain Torben, Ragnav, Freydis, you, and rooms for guests." She pointed at the last two rooms. The wooden doors were all open so she could see they were all unoccupied. Relief spread through her body. Torben was not here.

Her room was small and cosy. A comfortable-looking bed covered with warm pelts. A chest for her belongings. A stool, washstand, chamber pot, and a latticed window that let sunlight in. On the bed was a tray of food and her comb from Ragnav. She eagerly reached for it and started to tease out her tresses and Olga laughed.

"You fix hair, you eat, and you sleep. You wake when we eat later," Olga informed her and left.

She sat on the bed and alternated between combing her hair and eating the bread, cheese, and fruit. The room was clean and the floor had fresh rushes littered with sprigs of lavender. It was a much bigger space than she was accustomed to. As a handmaiden, she had slept on a makeshift pallet on the floor beside her mistress's bed. This room was a luxury, and she would have moments of privacy.

Wynflaed let out a shuddering yawn that wracked her whole body. She *did* feel exhausted even though it was daylight still, her body did not care. It had been many a night since her abduction from Northumbria. The journey to get here had been arduous and exhausting, with few opportunities to sleep peacefully. She had a whole new life to adjust to. She had made this choice and she had no regrets. She lay back on the bed and closed her eyes as the events flashed through her mind. Each thought led back to one person. Torben.

Chapter Twelve

Torben felt Ragnav, Leif, and Leif's brother, Sven, watching him pace back and forth. They had been counting coins—gold and silver—and taking inventory from the trade, but Torben could not sit still and focus like he normally would.

"What is wrong with Torben? I have never seen him so out of control," Sven asked with interest. Torben heard him ask the question and ignored it. It had been posed about him and not to him, anyway. "It is a woman that has addled him so," Leif offered, his brow furrowed.

"One of the freed women?" Sven asked, and his greyish-blonde eyebrows lifted in surprise.

"Yes. It is the one named Wynflaed. She has placed a spell on him. Or perhaps it is Loki, the trickster. He would delight in seeing our Torben, usually so controlled, blinded by lust."

"Ah, I see! He wants to bed her," Sven stated knowingly, as if that was all that needed to be said.

"No," Torben said in a firm tone. "It is not like that." He heard the defensive protest in his voice and knew he would not fool his cousins and brother.

"So, you have come to care for this Wynflaed? In such a short time? This may be fate," Sven offered thoughtfully.

"I have never seen Torben act the way he does around Wynflaed. I think he fell in love with her the moment he set his eyes upon her. I do not understand why he is not bedding her at this very moment," Ragnav said with a shake of his head.

Torben just let out a disgruntled sound. He did not yet understand his own feelings so how could he explain them to others? He threw his head back in frustration and growled at his foolishness. He should have not kissed her so soon, he wanted to give her time to adjust. He wanted to get to know her. But she responded so passionately she must feel something as well.

"See how his brain is addled," Leif said, gesturing to Ragnav and Sven. "He has been reduced to growling like a wolf, he cannot even speak." They all laughed and Torben glared at them.

"Get back to the task at hand!" A growl was still clear in his tone.

"Do not bite us, Torben. We will stop our jesting, but in seriousness, what of Gunhilda?" Ragnav asked him.

Torben groaned inwardly. He had forgotten about Gunhilda. He had caught a glimpse of her when he introduced the new settlers to the people of Klavik, but he was too distracted by Wynflaed. Gunhilda was a widow and had chosen to continue farming her husband's plot instead of remarrying. He had been a goat herder, and she continued to raise them, milk them, and supply their meat to the settlement. She also provided paid work for the adolescents while teaching them how to care for the goats.

Gunhilda was a free woman and one evening had approached Torben and whispered an invitation in his ear. He had deliberated, but eventually accepted after explaining he did not wish to marry. Neither did she, and a mutual relationship had started that was based on sexual gratification when the feeling struck them. He always went to her and she demanded nothing of him except his attention, but he had started to notice her jealousy whenever she spied him speaking with other women. He had meant to address it upon his return.

"I will speak with Gunhilda. As it stands, there is nothing between Wynflaed and I, so I expect you not to gossip like washerwomen when my back is turned."

All three men rolled their eyes at his accusation.

"Do not worry, Torben. We will only poke our fun at you when we are alone," Leif informed him with an innocent smile. Leif's fairness resembled his more than Ragnav, but he was slender in build and had a softness to his features so people called him pretty, which always made him scowl with distaste. What Norseman wanted to be "pretty"?

Torben decided there was no time like the present and went to seek out Gunhilda. He went to the stables and saddled his horse, Bein, ivory like her namesake. Bein was an Icelandic horse, sure-footed and agile. He had trained her well and they moved as one with his silent commands. Ragnav had been asking to branch out into breeding horses for sale and trade since they had strong mares ready for breeding and a colt that had now grown into a magnificent stallion. He was pleased Ragnav wanted to take on more responsibility and this could be something he cultivated on his own. *I will give him free rein.* He smiled wryly to himself as he tugged on Bein's reins.

He rode up the path to Gunhilda's farm and heard the cacophony of bleating goats. He heard Gunhilda talking to them, admonishing them for their impatience as she threw food out to them.

"Be still, wretched things, lest I make you all sacrifices to Odin." Fondness for her goats shone through in her empty threat.

"With how many goats you have, Gunhilda, Odin would certainly settle many blessings upon us," Torben called to her as he dismounted Bein. His horse was so well-trained there was no need to tie her to a post, Torben simply asked her not to move until he returned. Bein eyed the goats and snorted with derision but nodded, and Torben rubbed her neck in thanks.

"Come, let me pour you some mead, Torben. I missed you at my table," Gunhilda said with a sultry smile.

This will not be an easy conversation. He sighed to himself and followed her into the hut.

Despite her close proximity to the goats, her home always smelt clean. Fresh and dried sprigs of herbs and flowers hung from the rafters and a fire created wisps of smoke to circulate the scented bundles. He sat at her table and observed her as she prepared a mug of mead. She was an attractive woman, fair of skin and hair with pale blue eyes, a Norse woman through and through. Her figure was womanly and strong, evidence of her outdoor labour. She sat across from him and placed a flagon and two wooden mugs on the table.

"You seem distant, Torben. There is a faraway look in your eye," she observed as she searched his face.

"It was a long journey, Gunhilda. I am glad to be home."

"Yes, and you have brought guests?" she asked without looking at him, instead plaiting a loose tuft of hair.

"Yes, but settlers, not guests. They were about to be sold and I could not let that happen."

"Is that not what happens along the trade route? Don't they sell people?" she asked, meeting his eyes.

"They do, and I steer clear of those markets, but this one caught my eye. And it was Guthred who sold them."

"Ah, so Guthred made the choice for you," Gunhilda said, a little relieved.

"Yes and no. My mind was made up before he appeared," he said honestly. Her eyes narrowed.

"Well, we–the people of Klavik–will all welcome them," she said with forced cheerfulness.

"Yes, I am going to be very busy, ensuring they settle in. I need to spend more time with Ragnav and Freydis and start preparing for winter. It will give me no time for other pursuits."

He did not want to hurt her, but he would not shy away from the blunt truth.

"You mean warming my bed?" she asked him boldly.

"Yes. We both said this would not lead towards a marriage," he said in a gentle tone. He felt he now needed to justify what he thought had been a mutual understanding. The niggling feeling she wanted more poked at him and he cursed himself for not having realised it sooner.

She nodded and bit her lower lip. For a moment, he thought she would cry and despair clutched at his chest. He could never deal with a crying woman.

"You are right. We knew this would come to an end. And you are chieftain of our people. Of course your time will be consumed with family, preparations, and the settlers." There was a slight edge to her tone, but he saw no tears build up in her eyes and he felt relieved. *Coward.*

"I am glad you understand, Gunhilda. You are vital to our settlement, all the people of Klavik are grateful for you. Will you come feast with us? We will say thanks with celebrations and pay homage to the gods for another safe journey."

Chapter Thirteen

Wynflaed awoke, but her eyelids felt so heavy it took a few moments before she could open them. She felt slightly rested, but a little crabbish. Her body felt stiff and she stretched out her limbs in an effort to ease the soreness. She must have slept like the dead and not moved at all during the night to feel such stiffness. *I need another hot bath.* She sat up and looked over to see that the bowl on the washstand was full of water.

She went over and splashed it on her face. The cold water worked its magic, and she felt more alert as she picked up her comb to neaten her hair. The fresh, floral scent of the soap she had used lingered on her hair and skin. Her hair felt so soft. She lifted a curl to her face and saw the shine that bounced off the dark locks. Her hair, while short, was still long enough to easily reach her line of vision. She gave her head a shake, letting the curls fall where they may, and was ready to go out and explore. Back home her hair would normally be held up under a wimple. She did not miss wearing a headdress and found a freeness without it.

She carefully pushed open the door and peeked out to see Freydis leaving her room as well. Wynflaed made a little noise.

It was meant to be a throat clearing but came out as a squeak, and Freydis turned around with a faint smile.

"Wynflaed. For a moment, I thought there was a mouse behind me. Come, walk with me to the great longhouse for the feast." She extended her arm and Wynflaed linked hers with Freydis's with a polite nod.

She was much friendlier than Wynflaed had hoped for, as she thought back to their earlier introduction. Freydis seemed prepared to give her a chance. She knew she would have to earn her trust and make Freydis see beyond the scar because, in truth, Wynflaed had already seen past it. What she saw was a beautiful, insecure, and sad girl.

"Thank you, Freydis. I do not want to be a bother." She gave her arm a pat.

"From what Torben says, he wants you to be my companion, so it will not be a bother."

Wynflaed listened for any frustration or annoyance in her tone. It held none and so she relaxed.

"Companionship can be most enjoyable in my experience. I was a handmaiden back in Northumbria and I spent pleasant days with my lady," Wynflaed offered.

"Then why did you choose to come here and not go back to your home?"

It was a fair question and, while there was a logical answer, she knew some of it had to do with Torben. But she had no intention of sharing any of that with his sister.

"The journey home was dangerous and I would have risked falling prey to bad men again after being rescued by Torben."

Freydis nodded with genuine empathy.

"I would like to hear about your journey one day if you would like to share it with me. I am sure my face pales in comparison to what you all went through," she said with shame.

"Do not compare yourself to others, Freydis. We all have our crosses to bear. Do not trap yourself in thoughts of despair on top of despair."

"You are wise, Wynflaed," Freydis said with a soft squeeze of her arm.

Freydis and I are already coming to be friends.

They had left the longhouse that was to be her home and now walked to the great longhouse she had entered when they first arrived. She could hear the noise of celebration already. The air was filled with the scent of smoked meats and fish, and she could see the mead flowed freely. She knew heathens practised sacrifices to their gods and her stomach turned queasy at the thought.

"Will there be sacrifices, Freydis? Do I need to prepare myself for the sight of them?"

Freydis laughed. It was a sweet sound, and Wynflaed wanted to try to make her laugh more often.

"Come, Wynflaed, we are not barbarians. We do not slaughter animals and dance around painted in their blood. We at times make a blood sacrifice to the gods, but Torben, Ragnav and I do it privately together at a special place dedicated to Odin. We make sacrifices to others of course, to Njord, our God of the Sea, Frigga, our Goddess of the Earth, and Thor, our God of Battle, when the situation calls for it. But our family lineage has always held an affinity with Odin."

Wynflaed nodded, still a little queasy, but if she thought of it logically, it was no different than preparing an animal for a meal. The animal was slaughtered either way, but when sacrificed to the gods, its body was not eaten.

Wynflaed watched as people made way for Freydis, making every attempt not to stare at her face. *All that does is draw more attention*, Wynflaed thought angrily. But Freydis seemed accustomed to this behaviour, as her eyes held a detached look. When they entered the longhouse, Wynflaed saw rows of tables that spanned the length of the room that she had not noticed earlier. There were stools on either side, but she noted many people sat on the floor, especially some of the men already deep into their cups. Freydis led her to the head of a table close to the dais and sat down.

"Torben and Ragnav sit there," she said, pointing at the wooden chairs that looked like thrones. "That is where my parents sat, and my grandparents before them. Torben always offers to have a third chair made but I always refuse."

Wynflaed nodded. She understood her reason. She turned and caught the eyes of Hilde, Cola, and Cynewin, and gestured for them to come over. Cola, once he saw Cynewin was at ease, left to find some of the men he had become friendly with. Wynflaed, after she made introductions to Freydis, hugged Hilde and Cynewin and asked for every detail of their time apart. She had missed their company.

"I have found my place and where I feel most at ease, Wynflaed. Taking care of others, washing, mending, and learning different ways from the other women. Olga is highly skilled at many things, and I am willing to learn," Hilde told her with a contented smile. Wynflaed admired her sweet disposition. So very unlike her own, as she had recently discovered.

"Our hut is nice, Wynflaed, even nicer than back home. And Olga gave me a loom and asked me to show her what I can make," Cynewin said with a shy smile at having been given a personal task.

Her friends appeared joyous in this moment, and she hoped it would remain so, as she had guided them down this path. Wynflaed knew she would never set foot in Northumbria again, but with Hilde, Cynewin, and Cola, she would always have a piece of home with her.

She was about to share her own experiences but caught sight of Torben as he entered to a great cheer from his people.

He smiled and waved at them and accepted a mug of ale. Torben's eyes scanned the room, but his gaze stopped when someone grabbed his arm. Straining her eyes, she saw it was the woman who had gazed at her with disapproval when he had introduced them to the settlement earlier. Freydis, who had been watching her, spoke up.

"Torben has arrived with Gunhilda on his arm, it seems. They are bedmates." Wynflaed caught Freydis watching her and shrugged as if she did not care. But care she did! *That must be why he pulled himself away*! Wynflaed could not blame him. Where she was short, Gunhilda was tall. She had short curly dark hair and Gunhilda had long blonde hair in beautiful plaits. Torben caught sight of them and let Gunhilda go with a nod in their direction.

"Good eve ladies, you all look refreshed." He offered a warm smile and his eyes lingered on hers before he focused his attention on the group.

"Yes, we are settling in nicely. Olga is a blessing," Hilde confirmed.

"And you, Cynewin, do you have all you need?" he asked the young girl gently. Wynflaed silently clapped inwardly at his tact.

"Yes, we have everything, many thanks," she responded so softly it was almost a whisper, but her eyes met Torben's shyly.

"What of you, Wynflaed?"

Unlike Cynewin, she refused to meet his eye and instead smiled at something past his shoulder, as if she could see something more interesting.

"I am feeling well Torben, very well," she said with false cheer. She felt his eyes bore into her a moment longer before he moved to Freydis. She saw him place a kiss on her forehead from the corner of her eye.

"And you sister?"

"I feel happy to be in such pleasant company tonight, to

talk to these ladies of happy things and their joy to be here with us in Klavik."

His queries complete, he looked back to Wynflaed who still watched him from her peripheral vision.

"Enjoy the festivities! I will ensure either myself or Sven escort you *all* home."

Wynflaed knew this had been directed more at her than anyone else and she felt wildly irrational. She had a strong urge to stand on a chair to be as tall as he and shake her fist at him.

"Why do you look so fierce all of a sudden, Wynflaed?" asked Freydis.

Wynflaed looked back at her companions, who all watched her curiously.

"Nothing. I am fine, truly." She plastered a smile on her face and turned her focus back to them.

Chapter Fourteen

There was laughter, singing, and many a conversation around him, but Torben had blocked out all the noise when he focused his attention on Wynflaed. She was acting oddly this evening. She would not meet his eyes, and her responses had all seemed . . . unnatural. Very unlike her usual forthright self. The whole interaction had left him feeling disgruntled. All he wanted to do was pick her up, take her somewhere they could be alone, and kiss those maddening lips until she lost all her senses and forgot whatever she was mad about.

"Torben, are you with us?" asked Ragnav, who waved a hand in front of his face to try to gain his attention.

"What is it, Ragnav?" he said irritably, turning his head to his younger brother.

"You said you had something to share with me?" His smiling demeanour was unchanged by Torben's short tone. It was rare to find Ragnav in ill humour.

"I have considered your request to start breeding horses. I think it is a good idea. It shows me you are thinking, growing, and looking to make wealth outside of raiding."

He added the last part because he knew Ragnav was

frustrated by his limited raiding experience and had only gotten to hear the tales of heroes before him.

Ragnav nodded to show he understood the thinly veiled message, but he grinned excitedly at the prospect of pursuing his goal.

"Thank you, brother, thank you! I will not let you down. I have so many ideas, so many plans."

"I know you do. See Leif for any coin you need, and we will plot out some land to expand the stables. Ask Cola if he is interested. I watched him with the horses earlier and he has a natural skill with them."

Ragnav wasted no time and ran off to Leif. Torben smiled when Leif turned around with a scowl after Ragnav thumped him hard on the back to gain his attention.

He turned his awareness to the people who had lined up to talk with him and gestured them forward one by one to give them his ear. They brought him news of good harvests—carrots and cabbage in abundance—and crops of rye ready to be collected. Apples had also grown plentifully, and wild bilberries and hazelnuts had been foraged. One of his farmers brought bad news. A wolf, judging from the tracks, had attacked his herd of sheep twice, making off with two and leaving one dead. Torben patted the older man's shoulder in commiseration and offered the bulk of his newly returned men to hunt the wolf and watch over his herd at night till it was caught. The farmer's plot was close to the settlement and having a rogue wolf this close was a danger lest it get too confident and attack a human. Torben hailed Sven and gave him the news.

"Why did the old fool not tell me while you were gone?" Sven swore angrily.

"He told me he did not want to be a bother. I guess he needed to swallow some pride to ask for help at all, but he must have realised the situation had gotten out of his control." He tried to appease Sven who, like Leif, was quick to temper.

"I will make sure that his sons and a few other men are placed on the task, and I will oversee it myself."

Torben had been so busy with his people he had not set his gaze on Wynflaed in some time. When he realized this, he turned to where she had been, but he could not spot her. Freydis was still there, however, so he walked over to her.

"Where did Wynflaed go, Freydis?" He cut off her conversation with Hilde mid-sentence.

"She was overcome with tiredness and we urged her to go to bed."

"Alone?" he asked in a raised voice, which caused both Freydis and Hilde to jump.

"Yes, Torben. She knew the way back." Freydis frowned at his line of questioning.

"But I said I would escort you all home."

"Since when do I need an escort, Torben? Wynflaed is a strong-minded girl and she will be fine. And you have been busy."

He barely refrained from spitting out a vile curse in front of the women and calmed himself. He would go and ensure Wynflaed had returned safely.

"Thank you, Freydis," he said between gritted teeth and stormed out into the night.

He followed the path Wynflaed should have taken to reach the longhouse and did not spot her. *Perhaps she has already made it to her room*, he thought, as his feet led him to the door. He could hear movement inside and that should have been enough to allay his fears. But he wanted to see her, to hear her.

He tapped softly on her door.

"Wynflaed, it is Torben. I just wanted to check that all is well with you."

"I am well." Her terse reply did not deter him.

"I want to see it for myself."

Silence was her response, but a few moments later the door opened and they stood face-to-face.

"Yes, Torben, as you can see, I am fine. What is it that you need?"

The loaded question made desire shoot through his body, and he hardened with want. What he needed was her. She stood before him in a clean shift, one of much better quality and fit than she wore when he had first seen her. A candle was lit behind her, which created a shadowed silhouette of her luscious body. He could even see the faint dusky hue of her nipples through the fabric, the tips tightened under his perusal. It dawned on him that he was standing there not saying a word, just staring like a hungry beast. This need was beyond basic, she consumed all his senses.

He lifted a hand to cup her face and tried to calm himself. He was Chieftain, not a lusty youth.

"I just needed to know you were well, Wynflaed." His voice was husky as he stroked her soft cheek.

"I am fine, as you can see. I just need some more sleep. As do you, you were very busy all evening. I am sure that woman is waiting for you."

Confusion mixed into his lust. *A woman waiting for him?*

"What woman?" he demanded, as he searched her upturned face for a clue.

"The woman you arrived with."

Realisation dawned on him. *Gunhilda.*

"She is not my woman, Wynflaed. I have no woman." *Not yet,* he said to himself.

He was glad another woman had caused her jealousy and bit back a smile at his satisfaction.

"Can I interest you in my company on the morrow? I could show you around, introduce you."

Her face softened and she nodded.

"I will bid you good sleep and see you well rested on the morrow." He leaned down and gave her pursed lips a soft kiss. He felt the sharp intake of her breath. She was caught by surprise, but within a moment she returned his kiss and braced her hands upon his chest. He did not want to overstep, so he broke their embrace and pulled away. She was confused and her expression quickly turned to displeasure. He was met with a terse "sleep well" in return, and the door closed in his face. He grinned. *By the gods, I love her fire.*

Chapter Fifteen

Someone is calling my name, I must go to them, I must find them. Wynflaed dreamed she ran through a forest of gnarled trees and stumbled on snowcapped rocks.

"Wynflaed, are you well?"

Torben's voice, accompanied by firm raps on the wooden door, broke into her dream.

Oh, it was Torben. Oh, it was TORBEN!

"Is it morn already?" she called, and looked around the room. The small window allowed sunbeams to light the room and she immediately jumped to her feet.

"It is." She heard the smile in his voice and scowled.

"I will ready myself and meet you outside."

"As you wish."

She heard his footsteps as he walked away. Frantically, she attended to her ablutions and muttered self-deprecating oaths. Did she want to kiss those infuriating lips that left her in desperate want or slap the sensuous smile from his cocksure face? She had seen his grin before she had closed the door in his face the previous night and had fumed because he had seen her jealousy.

She threw on her clothes from the day before and ran a comb through her hair. She smoothed her hands over her dress and took a deep breath.

She entered the open area of the longhouse, looked around, and caught the eye of a young man who pointed towards the doorway. She gave him a smile and quickly walked outside. The first thing she saw was a raven, sitting on the wooden post of a drying rack. Its direct eye contact unnerved her but she could not break the gaze. The raven let out a squawk and took flight, making her start a little.

Mind your senses, Wynflaed, she scolded herself.

She found Torben waiting for her with a hunk of fresh baked bread and some hard cheese.

"I thought you might enjoy a repast as we walk and talk."

She took the offering with thanks and inhaled the delicious smell of the still warm bread before she tore off a hunk with her teeth.

She caught the gleam of Torben's white grin.

"Your appetite gives me joy, Wynflaed. I can truly say this is not an emotion I normally feel watching people eat."

"It must be my ladylike graces," she said dryly and flourished the bread and cheese in the air.

"I have much to learn about you."

"And I you, Torben. Where are we going first?"

Wynflaed's senses were overwhelmed. Torben had showed her so much of Klavik–and introduced her to so many people–she would need days for it to settle into her memory. They had seen food stores, craftsmen, seamstresses, fishermen, hunters, and livestock caretakers. There were farms and crops in each direction. The settlement was organised and ran smoothly. Everyone did their work with a smile–she was impressed. This could be a hard life, but Torben's people did not make it seem a miserable burden. She recalled those of equal standing back home, and in comparison the people here looked more content. He was a good man who lent a hand or kind word to all he passed, and she felt something she had never felt for another person, pride. This towering Viking who could cleave a person in two with his axe was also a sweet, kind man and she felt herself softening.

"Why do you look at me so gently, Wynflaed?" he asked with a cocked eyebrow.

"I just find it hard to believe that you are real at times. You are so like my captors in looks and the way you live." She swept her arm across the settlement. "But you and your people greeted me with warmth and made me feel safe."

Her confusion only deepened after she said the words out loud. Something visceral pulled her to this man. Something that went beyond gratitude or lust. She could see him every day and be content in his presence. Or even prickly, since he did not seem to mind that side of her. His gaze was thoughtful as he absorbed her words and considered a response.

"It is true that any man of the North–whether here or Jutland–who calls himself a Viking is known to many as a heartless heathen. I am a well-travelled, well-learned man. There are some of my kind, but there are many like Guthred. What I have learned is at our core we are all the same. We all bleed red. We all eat off the land. We all hurt, we all love–and we are all human. To place a lesser value on a person because of where they come from or their rank is not humane. And that is what I expect of my people if they wish to be in Klavik. And you, too, Wynflaed, when you are ready to stop seeing us as Vikings but instead as your people."

His words washed over her, powerful like a crashing wave,

but she felt warm inside like a roaring hearth. A shiver travelled up and down her spine and she nodded. She tried to think of words to parry his but she found herself speechless and stepped closer to grab his hand.

"I will. I feel no ill will toward you."

A mischievous smile spread across his face.

"And what of when I saw you last? You were as frosty as a winter morning."

She laughed and squeezed his hand, satisfied with the fluid movement from their heartfelt talk to light-hearted banter. Wynflaed was about to respond in kind when she saw Gunhilda headed towards them.

"What has caused that sour look?" Torben asked gently, as he rubbed his thumb over their still entwined hands. She had not led a pampered life, but her skin was creamy and soft, and he seemed to enjoy it.

His head snapped up when she spoke.

"It appears your woman has come to seek out your attention."

Chapter Sixteen

Torben was not proud to admit that he revelled in Wynflaed's blatant jealousy. Her tone was frostier than the snowcapped mountains. The connection he felt with her was not one-sided and he wanted everyone and everything else to fade away so he could explore it further.

But alas, Gunhilda is making her way to me with a determined look on her face. He turned to follow Wynflaed's gaze. She pulled her hand away and he felt the loss of her touch keenly. His hands flailed in the air, and he quickly moved them to his hips as he gave Gunhilda a nod.

"How do you fare today, Gunhilda? How are the goats?"

"All is well, Torben, and the goats keep me well amused with their endless singing."

Wynflaed and Gunhilda stared at one another. They both had wide, stiff smiles that did not quite reach their eyes.

"Please accept my apologies, I have yet to make introductions. Gunhilda, let me introduce Wynflaed of Northumbria."

Gunhilda nodded her head in greeting, her smile

unmoving. He cleared his throat at the growing tension and turned to Wynflaed.

"And this is Gunhilda. She, ah, she tends the goats."

"I gathered as much, Torben, when you asked how the goats were. I am pleased to meet you, Gunhilda."

Wynflaed gave a polite curtsey and smiled sweetly.

"Is there something I can do for you, Gunhilda?" Torben asked, attempting to move this awkward situation along.

"If you are free when the sun starts to set, I thought I could interest you in some mulled mead. I have a new brew I think you will enjoy."

Gunhilda's insinuation was not lost on Torben as she held his stare. The energy from Wynflaed's glower was so powerful he did not need to turn to see her reaction to the innuendo.

"I think not, Gunhilda. I will be occupied elsewhere." There was a tense silence so he cleared his throat, but all it did was heighten the awkwardness. Suddenly, Wynflaed stepped beside him and smiled at Gunhilda.

"Is there anything else we can do for you?" she asked with a polite authority.

Gunhilda's eyes blinked widely at the bold query. She looked between Wynflaed and Torben, exhaled, and drew herself to her full height.

"No, I think I have all I need to know. It was nice to meet you, Wynflaed. I bid you both farewell."

Torben turned and looked down at Wynflaed and a smile twitched on his face.

Her jealousy and possessiveness made his blood run hot and it meant Wynflaed held the same feelings for him. She had claimed him. As fierce as Freyja in war and love, his little termagant still glowered at him from behind her forced smile.

"Is this what I am to expect, Torben?" she demanded, hands on hips.

"What do you want from me, Wynflaed?" he asked softly. Actions were one thing. But he needed words.

"I want to know what that woman means to you."

"In truth, I have warmed Gunhilda's bed but that is all. My feelings beyond that are the same I feel for any of my people." He watched her absorb the information.

"And what of me?" Her voice was now soft, the ferocity gone.

"Since I laid my eyes upon you, Wynflaed, you have consumed my being. I yearn for you. Your thoughts, your touch, your fiery spirit. I want to know every inch of you, inside and out."

His words made her tremble, so he pulled her close.

"Do you shiver with fear or because you feel the same?" he whispered.

"I cannot make sense of it, Torben, but I feel the same." Before he could respond, she pressed herself up and kissed him hot and hard, her lips searing her claim.

She released his mouth and shook her head.

"Torben, this is absurd, you are a Chieftain, and I am a servant. All I can be is another lover to you."

"That is not how I see you! Nor what I expect!"

She stepped away and he felt powerless to stop her.

"I need to think all of this over, away from you."

"I will respect your space, Wynflaed." That was all he could bring himself to say. As he watched her walk away, he ruminated. This was the first time in his life he had felt so strongly for a woman and braved telling her and now he was left standing alone, feeling like a fool. A raven swooped down and sat near his feet.

"Ah, my friend. To have even a raven take pity on me makes this a very sad moment indeed."

Chapter Seventeen

Wynflaed sat with crossed legs under a birch tree that gave her a good view of the settlement. She bit into a ripe red apple with contentment. She had managed to avoid Torben the last three nights and had spent her days learning things about Freydis and the running of the Klavik settlement. Torben had stirred such a myriad of emotions in her when she last stood alone with him that any thought of him pushed her into a state of indecision. She licked a streak of apple juice from her hand that had dripped from the sweet flesh.

"You do not act like a high-born lady," Freydis commented. She sat opposite Wynflaed and observed her manner.

Wynflaed shrugged.

"I am not high-born, I was a handmaiden to a high-born lady," she reminded Freydis, and then nibbled the rest of the apple to the core before she tossed it in a basket of scraps for pig feed.

"Still, you are most unusual and I like it. Especially how outspoken you are."

Wynflaed grinned in return, knowing she referred to her

high-handed approach the last few days. While the people of Klavik respected and obeyed Torben, it was clear when he was away Freydis and Sven were not treated with the same regard. This problem mainly affected Freydis, since Sven spent his days ensuring the perimeter was safe and seeing to the manly tasks like hunting. Freydis was charged with the upkeep of the main longhouses, cleanliness, meal preparation, and keeping the stores well stocked. Freydis usually spent her time alone, withdrawn in her misery, and the settlement either took advantage of it or could not function without direction.

Wynflaed was unsure which it was–perhaps a little of both–but she had made it clear everyone needed to play their part. Her attitude had also rubbed off on Freydis who had slowly started to engage with her people again. The pair had stopped to assist the villagers while they made sure everything ran smoothly.

Wynflaed had to admit the Norse (she tried not to use the term Viking, for that conjured thoughts of men like Guthred) were very clean people, more so than the back home. Back home, bathing was a chore done every so often, and not by everyone. She had used rags and water to wipe herself clean between baths or, in warmer weather, the river. But some of her countrymen could go for an age without a proper wash–especially the lower class–and Wynflaed had always been grateful she spent most of her time with the upper class. The Norse, however, bathed almost every day in the bathhouses or a nearby river where another hot spring tempered the water.

Winter was coming, and she knew it would be colder than winters back home. She was soaking up all the sunshine she could now as she followed the rays throughout the day.

She and Freydis had just finished checking the grain stores and she debated whether they should check the salted fish stores or check in with Hilde and the other washer women.

They generally had an amusing titbit for her, as she had come to learn since her arrival.

"Wynflaed, do you mind sharing with me how you came to be here in Klavik? Or is the memory still too raw?" Freydis asked, interrupting her own thoughts of her path to Klavik.

"I can share it with you. It is not raw, nor will I forget. It is something that happened and I cannot change it, no matter how I feel. All I can do is look to the future," she said with emphasis. She never let an opportunity go to remind Freydis about acceptance, Wynflaed had caught her in sullen moods over the last few days, usually in the presence of Torben.

I can relate, Wynflaed said silently to herself.

Wynflaed began her story with the message from her ailing father and described the events through arriving in Kyivan Rus. Freydis's beautiful eyes widened with horror at their brutal capture, she smiled at Hilde's ingenuity, and was aghast at the events in Kyivan Rus right before Torben had appeared.

"Your brother was not a man to be trifled with. Even when the leader of this band of wretchedness came forward as a friend, Torben remained unmoved. I did find it curious that the man called him friend and referred to him as Torben 'Hel-Bringer'. All he said contrasted with the man–the saviour–that stood before us. But this leader, this Guthred, was intent on poking Torben's hard shell."

"Did you say Guthred?" Freydis cut her off sharply.

"Yes, Guthred. I do not know son of who or anything. He was almost as large as Torben and I remember he had small, evil eyes," Wynflaed said with a shiver. Freydis's eyes darkened to the shade of a stormy sea, deep blue and muddled, and Wynflaed began to feel uneasy.

"What is it, Freydis? Do you know of this Guthred?" she asked, even though the answer seemed clear.

"I do. I was to marry him until Torben forbade it." Her

voice was both hard and sad, as if she could not decide which emotion was stronger.

Taken aback by the knowledge, Wynflaed said the first words that sprung to her mind.

"You wanted to marry that brute?"

"He is not a brute!" Freydis shot back angrily.

"He planned on selling us, of course he is a brute!" Wynflaed declared. She stood her ground, shocked by the sudden change in Freydis's behaviour.

"I know it is wrong, but you do not understand. That is still a way of life for many." A pleading tone had now entered Freydis's voice. "Guthred is strong and sweet, he saw past my scars. He loved me for me."

Wynflaed said nothing for a few moments. They just stared at each other while they reeled from the revelations that had just sprung forth between them.

"And this is why you are mad at your brother?" Wynflaed asked softly, as understanding dawned upon her.

Freydis nodded and tears pooled in her eyes.

"He would rather keep me miserable here in Klavik than let me be with the man I love, and he never told me why. Only that he was Chieftain and that was his final word. And he sent Guthred away. He never even let me say farewell."

Freydis seemed so upset that Wynflaed bit her tongue. Freydis was not thinking straight. There was more to this story, and it was obvious nothing she said could convince Freydis that Guthred was evil. Only Torben could explain the truth to her.

"Come Freydis, do not fret so. Let me take you to your room so you can rest."

Chapter Eighteen

The swoosh of an axe split the air and cleanly cleaved the block of wood in front of Torben. Chopping wood was a favourite pastime for him. It was especially good for a moment of quiet meditation on his thoughts. Thoughts he was unable to control since they were all of Wynflaed. Subtlety was not her strong suit. Her purposeful avoidance of him was clear and all he could do was ask himself questions he didn't have answers to. Had he pushed her too far? Had his admission scared her?

He was so intent on the wood chopping and his thoughts that his instincts were slower than normal when he heard the leaves crunch. The noise was soft, so he knew it was a small person. They cleared their throat, and he knew who it was. His body sensed her and the reaction in his loins meant it could only be one person. Wynflaed.

He laid down the axe then turned around to meet her and was greeted by a sheepish look and crossed arms. Unsure but defensive. He offered what he hoped was a warm smile that would encourage her to break this silence.

"Wynflaed, I am very pleased to see you. Are you well?"

Her posture relaxed.

"Torben. I was wondering if we could talk. I know I have not been very—well—talkative of late." She half smiled and then bit down on her lower lip.

Relieved, he waved her admission off. She had missed him.

"Of course, let us go sit over here." He pointed to some stumps. "And I know I gave you cause for ire when we last spoke."

Wynflaed blushed and sat down.

"I went from feeling jealous, to kissing you, to pushing you away in quick succession," she said, not meeting his eyes.

He leaned forward, placed a finger under her chin, and turned her face to his. He wanted to be gazing deep into her eyes when he answered her.

"You did, and I have no judgement for either action. I have simply missed you and hoped our absence from one another made your heart grow fonder."

Wynflaed's eyes dropped to his lips, and he felt their heavy breath mingle, but then she shook her head and pulled back from him.

"I came here to talk about Freydis."

He nodded, now sensing that something to do with his sister troubled her.

"I see you have lifted her spirits greatly. The settlement has also responded to you in a welcoming way." He searched her face for a clue.

"Yes, they have. I am very relieved, truth be told. Freydis and I have grown close. We work well together, and we will provide you with an update on the stores. But Torben, I fear I distressed her when she asked me what happened in Kyivan Rus and I said the name Guthred."

The realisation hit, and he wanted to kick himself for having been so stupid. How did he not have the foresight to realise the matter of Guthred would arise between Wynflaed and Freydis? He had been too consumed by thoughts of

Wynflaed. Her scent, her touch, and that fiery spirit. Her face showed her impatience as she narrowed her eyes at him. She wanted an explanation, and she wanted it now.

"Wynflaed, I gather you learned Freydis is furious with me because I forbade her marriage to Guthred. Rest assured. I have my reasons."

"Which are?" Her response surprised him. After her experience, he had assumed it would be quite clear.

"He is not a good man. You saw him." He heard the exasperation in his own voice. "I was protecting her."

She nodded, seeming to accept the response.

"Why have you not explained it to her in this way, or shared with her how you came to save me?"

"She will not hear of it. And it will upset her more. It is easier for her to be mad at me than feel shame and regret that she wanted to marry the man."

"I think what she needs is the harsh truth, unpleasant as it may be."

"If that is what you suggest, I shall do it. I trust your judgement."

Wynflaed covered his hands with her own.

"I have missed speaking with you. Being close in your company."

"Have you thought more about what I said to you?" She must hear the eagerness in his voice.

"I have, Torben, and I was wondering, what kind of man would you say you are?"

Her voice was slightly husky, and he realised they had once again drawn close. He could feel the heat that emanated from her body as his own pulse started to thud.

"I am a man who wants to consume every part of you, Wynflaed. Your heart, your body, your soul."

Throwing sense to the wind, he pulled her against his chest and kissed her hungrily. He had no restraint, which felt foreign since he prided himself on self-discipline. He plundered her mouth with his tongue and his hands swept the soft curves of her body. He felt like an animal. His primal instincts had overcome any rationality and, as she rubbed her body against his, her ardent response only fuelled his desire.

"I need you, Wynflaed. I need to be one with you," he panted breathlessly to her.

I need her like I need my next breath of air.

Chapter Nineteen

They were very much alone. She had not thought further about being in such close proximity to him after avoiding his presence. Her body flushed with heat and desire as she inhaled his scent of crisp air and hard-earned sweat. She tried to stay focused and to stop her gaze as it travelled down to his lips, as she imagined them pressed against her body. She tried to keep her eyes on his torso, but then all she could see were the bulging muscles that rippled across his chest and arms. The intensity between them meant he wanted her, too. Knowing it and hearing it were two different things, though. Hearing those words leave his mouth unleashed the wanton in her.

"Take me, Torben. I want to be yours. I want you to be mine."

She stood back from him and slipped off her cloak, then pulled down her gown till she was in her shifts and boots. His eyes darkened with desire, and it emboldened her to slip the shift down her body and take off her boots until she stood naked. The days had begun to cool as winter neared, but she burned with passion and felt no chill as she ran her hands down her body.

"Take your clothes off, Torben, and lay upon the grass," she told him with no hesitation. Wordlessly, he obeyed and began to remove his own clothing till he, too, stood nude. She marvelled at the hard lines of his body. He was not just fair, but golden, his skin glowed in the setting sunlight that peeked through the clouded sky. She moved her gaze down his chest and gasped at the sight of his manhood aimed at her, big and hard. This was nothing like the previous encounters she had had. Before she lost her nerve, she moved to him and splayed her hands through the light sprinkle of fair hairs across his chest.

"My body yearns for you, Torben."

His response was a growl. No words, just a carnal sound as he swooped her up and gently laid her upon the grass. He rolled over so she was atop him. She felt the throb of the hardened proof of his desire against her own wet core and could not resist rubbing herself against him. He groaned and moved his hands from the thighs that straddled him up to the curve of her waist to cup her breasts. They ached for a touch she did not know was possible. She cried out in ecstasy when he raised himself up to take the tightened nipple in his mouth and suck. She had no idea this act could be so sensual, so gratifying, as he moved between each breast, suckling and rubbing.

"Are you ready for me, Wynflaed? I can feel the wetness of your need on me." He slipped a hand between her legs to her throbbing core. He placed his fingers inside her, one, then two, mimicking the consummation she desperately needed, and she rocked back and forth on his hand as she moaned his name repeatedly. She wanted him inside her, but the magic he worked with his fingers had gripped her body like she was possessed. He urged her to take her pleasure, and her body tensed all over as the most intense feeling of satisfaction spread through her body. The moment she had shared with herself was nothing compared to this, and she cried out. She lost the strength to stay upright and fell against his chest as she tried to steady her breath. Torben ran his hands through her hair and whispered words of sweetness. She had taken her pleasure, but what of Torben? She could still feel his hardness and sat back up.

"Only if you are ready, Wynflaed," he said gently with a pained expression.

"I am ready, Torben. I am not a virgin," she whispered and she closed her eyes. She moved her hand to stroke him, still amazed by the size. Her small hand could not fit around him as she positioned herself over him. She sank down, taking him slowly bit by bit until she was full of him. She opened her eyes to watch his face as she made her descent and was fascinated by the myriad of passionate expressions that passed across his face. Then he began to move, and she lost any conscious thought as rapture overtook her once again.

Chapter Twenty

Torben felt like he had died and the Valkyries had carried him to Valhalla. Surely this was what entering the Great Hall must feel like. A feeling of absolute bliss. Being one with Wynflaed was his Valhalla, she would be his everlasting bliss. He had easily pushed aside his jealousy at knowing he was not the only man who had known her. *I will be the last man that ever does*, he thought as he gripped her hips. She undulated on him as he thrust deep inside her. He wanted her to reach her peak again, and he used every bit of restraint he could muster to keep himself from his release. She was a vision of beauty with her head thrown back, her lush mouth parted as she moaned, and her hands grabbing her own breasts. Just when he felt he would burst, he felt the warm walls that gripped him tightly clench as she cried out again, and her whole body shuddered in release.

"Wynflaed, you are mine. Mine, Wynflaed. All mine," he growled at her between clenched teeth as he erupted inside her. Never in all his time had it felt this good. Her body collapsed on him, and he watched the last rays of the day fade.

It would be dark soon, but he did not want to leave her body and she did not seem to want that either.

'Wynflaed, are you well?" He hoped he had not been too ferocious in their lovemaking.

"I am more than well, Torben," she said with a sated voice, and looked at him with soft eyes. The amber colour was molten, warm, and deep, and he pressed a kiss to her forehead.

"I meant what I said to you, Wynflaed. You are mine now. Always."

"And you are mine, Torben. I will not share you with another." He bit back a smile at the fire that flashed through her eyes.

"I need no one but you, my spitfire love. They may call me Torben 'Hel-Bringer,' but you are a fire all on your own, Wynflaed.

"Speaking of which, I want to know you, Torben. Unburden yourself, tell me of who you were. I know who you are. And then we will discuss Guthred and Freydis."

He nodded. There could be no secrets between them.

"I will start with 'Hel-Bringer.' When I was younger, I fought in many battles. Against other Vikings, the foreign people of the faraway lands we raided, and your very own people. My grandfather sailed with Ragnar Lodbrok west. I was a young boy, of twelve summers. When they returned, they brought riches, a wealth of gold and silver, and slaves."

"The times when the Vikings learned that sailing west was possible, new riches and spoils was momentous, and as you know that they continue to do so to this day. Once I reached fifteen summers my father took me raiding. For practice, he said we would start with the Germanic tribes, people we have raided and fought with for generations. My father told me that when the battle began—once I had broken free from a shield wall—I was unstoppable, like I had the blood of a berserker. I would leave a path of destruction in my wake and come out untouched myself. I could never explain how I did this. Just that my senses were heightened, and my body was fluid with the axe and sword like we were one. I always felt Odin fought with me, I sensed his presence in my mind like my own thoughts were one with his. When I finally told my father, he was pleased. Our lineage had always held an affinity with the Raven God and I had been touched with a blessing not seen in the last few generations of our family. Of course I was proud. I was young, strong, and eager to share my reputation, so I began the journey to raid in the west."

"This means you received the name 'Hel-Bringer' when you arrived in my homeland," Wynflaed commented, her face still grim, but he saw a flicker of sympathy in her eyes.

"Yes, on the battlefield the men were in awe of my fighting skills and all the people I sent to the underworld. The goddess Hel, daughter of Loki, presides over Hel in Niflheim. They would say death sent them to Hel, a place for those who died without honour, without any heroic deed to their names. But to die by my hand meant that, even if you deserved it, Valhalla–or wherever the good Christians went–would not be for you. They whispered that that was my curse. I had Odin's spirit with me and he wanted the souls sent to Hel, and Hel would welcome them into her everlasting icy depths." His voice was hollow with the memories of all the death he had caused as he looked down at the ground. *I am not worthy to bask in her gaze.*

"But something made you step away from this, Torben," Wynflaed said gently, as she rubbed his hand in comfort. He raised his eyes back to her and saw compassion in her eyes, the sun' setting rays highlighted the golden flecks. He pressed her hand to his mouth and kissed it.

"I would fight in battles against men, but I always distanced myself from raids on villages. For a while I was indifferent and no one dared question me. The men were afraid to anger me lest they, too, be denied Valhalla and instead be greeted by Hel.

"There was one raid where I was overseeing the plundering of supplies, riding through the village to make sure nothing had been missed. As I rode by, I saw such atrocities committed, it sickened my stomach. I will not share what I saw, these visions do not belong in your mind. I rode away even though every instinct told me to strike my brethren down. I found a tree and carved a raven in it. I sliced my hand with a blade and pressed my bloodied palm upon the bird. I do not know why I did it, I suppose I thought it would help bring Odin to me. And it did. In my mind I saw Yggdrasil and Odin stood underneath it. He was cloaked but I could sense him. I asked for his forgiveness and for permission not to battle unless it was to defend my people. He nodded and said raiding was not my path any longer, and instead I could preserve the ways of old. He did not explain further, but the ways of my people had been to trade and farm, not just raid and plunder. I never lost the name 'Hel-Bringer,' it is a reminder of my part in the harm we caused. I will fight now to protect those I care for and when there is no other choice. It took my father a long time to accept, but I am glad he did before he passed. He knew I would protect Klavik and my siblings. That was enough for him."

Torben could not remember the last time had spoken this many words in a single sitting, and a huge weight lifted from his chest as he took a full breath of air. Wynflaed's face was contemplative as she watched him.

"Torben, what you did took more strength than needlessly killing and destroying everything in your path. I grew up hearing the stories of what was done to my people and it struck terror in all of us. You are brave. You are kind. Above all else, you are selfless, and you need to forgive yourself," she told him, her own voice now thick with emotion as she pressed both her hands on his chest.

"I try my best to make amends, Wynflaed. That day I saw you in Kyivan Rus, I think I knew you would be my salvation."

"Kyivan Rus. Guthred. Torben, now that I know you and what happened, how does it relate to Freydis?"

Torben narrowed his eyes.

"Guthred was the one who committed the atrocities that turned me away from battle. I will never allow my sister to wed that savage animal. She thinks it is love because she cannot see past her scar. Guthred is cunning and cruel. He wants to ally himself with our family, he always told me we would be an unstoppable force. When I left on a trading mission, he was welcomed in Klavik because I had never shared my dislike for him, and while he was here he won Freydis's heart. I forbade their union and sent him away and she is yet to forgive me."

"Did you explain to her what you just told me?"

"No, she does not need to know. I am her brother–her Chieftain–and she needs to trust me." He stood up and brought Wynflaed to her feet as well.

"Let us return to the settlement. Let us bathe and eat. And tonight you will be in my bed, where you will be for the rest of your nights."

Chapter Twenty-One

Wynflaed held Torben's hand while they returned to the settlement. It felt perfect. Large, calloused, and comforting. Only the thought of Freydis's situation could ruin this moment. Wynflaed knew how heartbroken she still was, and she needed to find a way to reach her without sharing what Torben had confided in her. Wynflaed was confident she could bring Freydis around eventually, no matter the limitations on what she could divulge. Freydis had lacked anyone to talk to about this and her emotions were pent-up and raw, but she would see sense eventually. Torben had bared his heart to her and given her a glimpse of his tortured and redeemed soul. She held no judgement for what he had done, only admiration for who he had become.

They soon arrived at the bathing huts. The area was lit with torches, but it was still dark enough to make it hard to recognise anyone. The few people around recognized Torben, of course, since he was their Chieftain and had an impressive stature and bulk. She could imagine their curious expressions but shrugged them off. She realised she cared naught for what anyone thought, a far cry from Northumbria and any concern of tarring her reputation. Here, she felt empowered to make choices that mattered to her and no one else.

Torben led them inside one of the huts and began to undress her. She stood there obediently and watched his eyes darken with lust as he revealed her skin, bit by bit. His adoration of her heightened her own passions, knowing she aroused him so. Once she was naked she pushed his hands away, so he began to remove his own clothes. She helped, and sneakily kissed each revealed patch of flesh, and she smiled when she felt his breath quicken. He had scars everywhere—small, jagged ones, deep gashes —and she traced them all, the healed skin raised but smooth, evidence of his warrior prowess. She pressed a kiss to his manhood, marvelling that the skin was so soft but so hard as he pulsated with need.

"Wynflaed," he choked out in a ragged breath as she explored brazenly. Her tongue glided along the length of him.

She instinctively opened her mouth, and he groaned while she moved her head back and forth, using a sucking motion and her hands to pleasure him. His hands tightly grasped her hair as he pushed into her mouth. Wynflaed grabbed his bare buttocks to steady herself, enjoying the act as much as he did.

He growled and pulled her away, then lifted her up to kiss her as he ran his hands wildly over her body. She wanted him to take her but was unsure how he could in this limited space. *Maybe I can straddle him in the water*, she thought desperately as he lashed his tongue over her breasts.

Torben had his own plan, so he turned her around and pressed her hands to the wall.

"You make me wild with need, Wynflaed," he growled as he entered her from behind. This new position was too much, though her wetness engulfed him eagerly. He planted his hands firmly on her hips as he moved in and out of her, and she rocked back enthusiastically as her body started to ascend to the peak of pleasure only he could make her feel. Within moments, they reached it together and cried out in unison. Her legs shook in the aftermath and Torben lifted her into his arms, walked over, and placed her in the bath. He joined her with the soap, and they took turns washing each other. She giggled as he washed her hair. He was so serious, biting the tip of his tongue that poked out as he massaged her scalp. Her hair was slowly growing, and she grinned at the idea of having him to wash it for her now, since it was a tedious task.

After they had rinsed off, dried themselves, and redressed, her stomach decided to alert them to the fact she was famished with a grumble that echoed through the bath hut.

Torben threw his head back and laughed, it was a beautiful sight. She watched his joy with adoration.

"Come, Wynflaed, your belly is saying it needs to be fed."

Instead of going to the main long house, they returned to the family house and sat at the table to eat. Leif was there going over the books and rolled his eyes when they walked in, hand in hand.

"I knew this would happen," he said with a shake of his head, but Wynflaed could see his smile.

"Never look a gift of foresight in the mouth, Leif," she retorted, but smiled as well. Torben called for food and, in a moment, stew, bread, cheese, and fruit were placed before them. Torben and Leif watched her heartily eat two bowls of stew in quick succession.

"We will need to increase our food storage for winter," Leif joked.

He caught the apple Wynflaed aimed at him, took a bite, and grinned at her.

"Did you see Freydis today, Leif?" Torben asked.

"When it was still daylight, yes. She told me she had womanly ails and would be in her bed for the rest of the eve and to not disturb her till morning," he said with a grimace, likely at his mention of womanly ails.

Wynflaed thought that was odd, since Freydis had not mentioned to her that she had received her flux or shown any signs of discomfort earlier today. *Or perhaps that's why she was in such an upset state?* She would discuss it with her tomorrow and added it to her mental list of items to discuss. She wanted Freydis to know she could talk to her about anything. She tried to stifle a yawn when a wave of tiredness washed over her body, but Torben saw it.

"Off to bed we go, Wynflaed. It has been an exhausting day for us both," Torben told her, as he reached out and kissed her forehead. She threw another apple at Leif who snorted at the word "exhausting" and followed Torben to his room. *Our room, I should say*, she thought happily, as she stepped over the threshold to her new life. Torben was hers, her Viking saviour.

Chapter Twenty-Two

Torben did not realise how exhausted they both were until they had lain upon the soft furs. His bed–which normally felt too big, even for his large frame–now felt right with her beside him. Wynflaed was the perfect piece he had not known he was missing. Mentally and physically replete, she had curled up against the length of his body and fallen asleep. He felt her slow, even breaths against his chest while she slumbered peacefully, and he stroked her silky hair mindlessly. He was tired, but his mind continually relived the events of the day. She had healed a wound deep inside him.

Sharing his past as a warrior and his role in Freydis's heartbreak with Wynflaed had lifted a heavy burden that he had carried for many years. She was the woman he saw himself growing old with, raising children with. Their souls had connected before their minds or their bodies had, and now they could spend forever learning one another. Though the events that had led him to find her were unfortunate, this was the plan of the gods and all the adversity only made them stronger. He leaned down to press a kiss on the top of her head, and pride swelled in his chest when he remembered standing up to Hakkan in the marketplace. Gut-wrenching fear quickly overshadowed pride when he thought of what could have happened if their paths had not crossed that day.

During all their lovemaking and baring of his soul, he had forgotten to bring up marriage. *They will be the first words I say to her when she wakes,* he promised himself. He stifled a yawn with his free hand and knew he needed to get some rest himself. He had a lifetime with Wynflaed, so he said a silent prayer of thanks to Odin, knowing the All Father was always nearby.

A loud gurgling noise slipped into Torben's sleep-filled mind, and he sat up with a start, looking around for his dagger. He heard giggling and he looked down to see a laughing Wynflaed.

"Calm yourself, Torben. It is just my stomach letting us know it has been sometime since we fed it."

Torben threw his head back and laughed with her.

"I have been awoken with less fear by the noise of battle," he teased, enjoying the early morning exchange. His mornings were usually a mundane repetition of routine.

"Come now, I worked up a healthy appetite, don't forget," she said with a blush, as she looked up at him through her eyelashes.

"Do not be embarrassed, Wynflaed, you were everything I had never even hoped to dream and more," he told her tenderly, and placed a kiss on her bare shoulder.

"I was just very...very...wanton. What must you think of me?" she murmured. Her eyes were still downcast, but he saw a soft smile at her words.

He placed his finger under her chin and raised her head so their eyes met.

"Wynflaed, what I think is I am a lucky, lucky man to know you in that way. And what I also think is you must marry me."

Her eyes widened in surprise.

"You want to marry me?"

His forehead wrinkled. He was taken aback by her question.

"Yes, I want us to be married. I want you to be my wife, and I your husband. To have children and grow old together."

He scanned her face, now pensive, and her pert nose crinkled as she eyed him curiously.

"It does not matter to you that you were not the first man to lie with me?" she queried.

"I am jealous at the thought of any other man touching you. But it does not bother me that I was not the first."

"I have no wealth or title. I come from a lower class in Northumbria," she pressed, and he could not help but let his exasperation show.

"Yes, Wynflaed, and none of that matters to me. I do not wish to marry a title or a chest of gold. I need none of that. What I need is you, you vexing woman." He claimed her lips in a hot kiss.

She responded with such ardour that he knew her answer would be yes. Her belly protested again with a gurgle and they broke apart laughing.

"Yes, Torben, I will marry you. But you better feed me before I change my mind," she said cheekily, but he saw soft tears pool in her eyes. He kissed each eyelid, tasting the salty wetness.

"You will not be sorry, Elskling." He moved off the bed to stand and pulled her up as well. "But we better wash and dress so I can feed you before I am sorry. Your tummy sounds ready for battle."

He broke into laughter at the indignant expression on her face at his jest. He had not felt this much lightness in many, many years.

Sven, Leif, and Ragnav's attention lifted from their plates of food when they walked in with linked hands. Sven paused with a chunk of bread halfway to his mouth. Leif had paused mid-chew, and whatever he had been eating was now visible as his mouth gaped open. Ragnav smiled widely and raised his cup in a congratulatory gesture to the two.

"Skol, Torben! Skol, Wynflaed!" he said enthusiastically.

Sven recovered and echoed Ragnav.

"Skol! It was only a matter of time! I cannot remember the last time I saw you this happy, Torben. Odin's blessings to you, Wynflaed," he told them with genuine warmth.

Torben looked to Leif, who was still frozen. Ragnav whacked him on the back and Leif spat out the food in his mouth involuntarily and looked over at Ragnav with a glare.

"I am just surprised, that is all. It is not every day you see Torben holding hands and Wynflaed... Well, Wynflaed, you are very...loud?"

Torben could not hold back his laughter at Leif's struggle to find words and very much enjoyed the scowl Wynflaed threw back at him.

"I am so pleased to see your happiness for us, Leif," she told him hotly.

Leif flushed and looked between Torben, Sven, and Ragnav before he let out a loud, somewhat tortured sigh.

"Welcome to the family, Wynflaed," he said dryly, with an embellished wave of his arm.

"Thank you, cousin. Speaking of family, where is Freydis?" he asked as he looked around the room. The men all shrugged in response.

"She seemed to be in one of her darker moods when I last saw her yesterday," Ragnav informed him, unconcerned by Freydis's changeability.

Wynflaed placed a steaming bowl of porridge in front of Torben, covered with bilberries and drizzled with honey. He grinned at her when she placed an equally large portion in front of herself.

"Considering what she and I spoke of yesterday, Torben, I think it is best I find and speak with her," she told him with a pointed stare.

"What happened yesterday?" asked Ragnav.

"Yes, what happened?" Leif and Sven echoed in unison.

The three bulky Norsemen looked to Wynflaed and Torben grinned. She was slight compared to them, but they all seemed to shrink under her watchful gaze.

"I shall leave the story to you, Elskling," he said.

Chapter Twenty-Three

Wynflaed held the attention of the whole table as Sven, Leif and Ragnav waited for her to answer the question. She looked to Torben, who nodded for her to continue.

"Freydis asked me about the events that led me to be here, and in sharing this tale with her, I divulged the name Guthred. She then shared with me her tale."

Leif and Ragnav groaned in unison.

"She must be steeped in a very black mood. You are right. We should find her. I will. You and Torben finish eating," Sven offered. He stood and pointed to Ragnav and Leif.

"You two, with me."

Wynflaed found herself alone with Torben again and she leaned over and placed a kiss on his cheek. A smattering of bristly hair tickled her mouth.

"What was that for?" he asked before he returned her kiss. She tasted fruit and honey on his lips, so she pulled closer and threw her arms around his neck.

"I am worried I will soon wake up from a dream, Torben. Being with you seems too good to be true."

"Trust me, Wynflaed, this is real. My love for you is more

real to me than anything else. More real than this food we eat, this air we breathe. You are my all."

She released his neck so they could finish eating and pondered the word love and what it meant. It was not a feeling she could have explained herself, but the simple way he explained it made all the sense she needed. *This wonderful man loves me*, she thought as she savoured the last few warm mouthfuls of her repast. She needed to find Hilde and Cynewin, they would share her joy. And Freydis. She hoped she would, too. They were becoming close, closer then Freydis and Torben were right now, and perhaps she could be the salve they needed to mend their broken past.

"Should I be concerned, Elskling? You look so deep in thought," Torben asked with mock worry as he stroked her hair gently.

She ignored his question and gave him a deep roll of her eyes. "What does that word mean?"

"It is an endearment, like darling. Do you like it?" He tugged on a strand of hair.

"I like it very much. I need to think of something to call you, I shall take my time in coming up with the perfect name." She tapped him on the nose with her finger, her smile impish.

"I need to do my duties around the settlement, Elskling. What will you do today? Can you come with me?"

"I must find Hilde and Cynewin. And I hope to find Freydis, partly to share the news with her, but more so to see how she fares."

Wynflaed felt dread in the pit of her belly when she thought of Freydis. *Something is not right.*

Torben raised his hand to her face and she felt his fingers gently brush her cheek.

"What troubles you, Wynflaed?" His blue eyes searched her face.

"The more my mind wanders to Freydis, the more a troubling sense of unease brews."

Torben's brow furrowed as he nodded.

"I share your unease, but we are both vigilant people, Wynflaed. It could just be our heightened senses."

Wynflaed forced a smile to spread across her face. He was right, and they had the choice to either feed into each other's fears or pray for the best. Whichever fate came to be, they would be side by side.

"Wynflaed, how nice to see you looking so well. Your skin glows when you are happy, did you know that?" Hilde exclaimed as they embraced.

"I did not, but I will not contest the matter because I am indeed very happy Hilde. Torben and I are in love!"

"I knew this would happen, my child. There was a fiery passion, fierce as a tempest, between you both. During that moment in the market, something passed between you and Torben and it bonded you, fated the love you share. Perhaps it was the works of their gods, as un-Christian as it is for me to say. But our forebearers also believed in many gods once, and who knows? Perhaps they are all the same. What I do know is a love like yours will go from strength to strength but only if you overcome challenges together, my child."

Wynflaed was awed. These were the most words she had ever heard Hilde speak and they had an undeniable wisdom veiled in warning and hope, whether intended or not. A shiver ran up and down Wynflaed's spine when she heard birds squawking. She looked up and saw a raven in the closest tree. It held her gaze before it took flight.

"Wynflaed, are you well? I did not mean any harm in my words," Hilde asked fretfully.

"No, no, Hilde. Your words were beautiful and heartfelt, I took no offence," Wynflaed assured her. "It just made me think of Freydis. We have not seen her today, and it could be nothing to be alarmed about, but I also have a sense of dread. Have you seen her, Hilde?"

"No, no, I have not, but I will help you look. Let us go ask Cynewin."

Wynflaed linked arms with Hilde. Her touch provided motherly comfort as they walked together to Cynewin and Cola's hut. The settlement was abuzz as it normally was at this hour. Lots of work, lots of noise. It was all normal, yet Wynflaed's foreboding grew.

Cynewin sat outside her hut with her loom. Her smooth brow wrinkled in concentration as she bit on her lower lip. She strung the threads firmly but gently and Wynflaed hated to interrupt her, so she placed a finger to her lips to signal Hilde to stay quiet and wait. When Cynewin finished the section, her face broke out into a pleased smile.

"It looks lovely, Cynewin. You have a true talent," Wynflaed said.

"Oh, Wynflaed, Hilde," Cynewin said with pleased surprise as she looked up. "Come, sit. Can I offer you refreshment?"

Cynewin clearly revelled in having a place of her own. Sooner or later Cola would marry and that would sadden Cynewin, so Wynflaed promised herself to keep her in this hut until she was ready to wed as well. They sat down together and Wynflaed began to share her news about Torben, which drew happy squeals from Cynewin. She threw her arms around both Hilde and Wynflaed. There was great strength in her small frame and Wynflaed laughed.

"Your joy for me warms my heart, Cynewin. We have all

been blessed following the moments of darkness we endured. But I also came to find you and ask a question–have you seen Freydis?"

"Why no, I have not. Is all not well?"

Wynflaed saw the panic flare in Cynewin's dark brown eyes and decided not to share any more with her. There was no point in upsetting another when Freydis could be home any moment.

"No, no, not at all. I have not crossed path with her today, is all." She squeezed the young girl's hands in assurance.

"Perhaps she is praying, finding a moment of solace with her gods. She likes to do that when she wants to be alone," Hilde offered.

Why didn't I think of that?

"That is true, Hilde, thank you. I will leave you both to your day."

She picked up the folds of her skirts and hurried towards where she knew the Ulfsons worshipped the gods. Freydis had shown her on one of their walks, and it was not too far from the settlement. She was on the outskirt of the settlement that led into the woods and shortly she would turn to the west and see the three large rock formations, the stone etched with faces of Odin, Thor, and Freyja. As she neared, she could see straight away Freydis was nowhere in sight, but the stones seemed to call to her so she approached cautiously, feeling the air thicken the closer she got.

The rock in the middle was the largest and the carvings on it depicted Odin, with Freyja and Thor to his sides. Wynflaed heard a squawk and looked up to see a raven overhead that landed to perch on Odin. She eyed it warily. She did not care much for birds with their beady eyes and sharp beaks. And this one made eye contact. The air still felt thick and she observed the offerings. Fruit and flowers for Freyja, mead and weaponry for Thor. Odin got all of that and more intricate wood carvings of runes, painted ravens on cloth, and a shield with the Ulfson's clan raven. There was also a deep bowl with feathers poking out and she inspected it closer to find a chicken–neck slit–and its blood pooled at the bottom.

Someone has been here recently to make a sacrifice.

"Was it Freydis?" she asked the raven, feeling silly for talking to a bird.

It gave her a look that spoke volumes. Freydis had been here and now Freydis was gone.

Chapter Twenty-Four

Torben cursed his luck as he scanned his surroundings, hand shielding his eyes.

Where was Freydis?

He had slowly started to realise that Freydis was no longer in the settlement. As he spoke to his people one by one and heard reports from Ragnav and Leif, it became clearer. Freydis had run away. Someone would have seen if she had been taken. But to run away without anyone noticing? That Freydis could do. She knew the settlement inside and out. Torben began to pace while he tried to piece it together. It was unlikely she had gone on foot, but none of the horses were missing. Ragnav had checked.

"Torben, I have news. Not good, I am afraid," Leif said regretfully as he ran over. "I went through Freydis's room and things are missing; her clothing, comb, and jewellery."

"She was more upset than we realised. How did I miss this?"

The settlement was his responsibility, but his family—his blood—was his life.

"You cannot blame yourself, Freydis oft fell into dark

moods. They came and went as did the sun and moon every day," Sven offered as he came in behind Leif.

His cousins offered words of comfort and logic, but even he could see they were worried.

"Actually, Torben, you know who we have not asked? Gunhilda," Ragnav said slowly, "She keeps a few horses and if you make your way past her home you leave the settlement behind."

Ragnav was right! But what would Gunhilda's role in this be? She and Freydis were not particularly close.

"I must find Wynflaed and gather supplies. I think you are right, Ragnav. She and I will go to Gunhilda's and from there we will follow her tracks."

Ragnav nodded and went to speak, but Leif cut him off.

"Should one of us not come with you?"

Torben shook his head. "I will not be parted from Wynflaed. And I want you and Ragnav to wait two sundowns before pursuing—Freydis may come back, but if she does not, you can catch up to us. Sven will take care of the settlement."

All three men nodded without any further questions.

"Torben! Torben, I believe Freydis has run away," Wynflaed said, running up to him. As soon as she was close enough, he pulled her into his embrace.

"I know, we are of the same mind. I want you and I to follow her. Let's pack supplies. Ragnav will ready horses for us. Can you ride?"

"I can make do. I will be coming with you regardless." She tugged at his tunic with fierce determination.

The gesture made his heart swell with pride at his feisty Valkyrie. They shared one thought, one mind. They were each other's equals. He bent down and pressed a hard kiss to her forehead.

"Come, let us prepare."

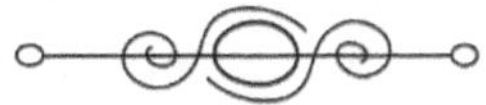

Torben had tasked Olga with gathering food supplies while he and Wynflaed packed belongings. It was especially cold at night, and they needed to ensure they kept warm. He grinned while she laid out her supplies on the floor, speaking out loud.

"Comb, soap, underdress, eating knife, woollen hose..." Her muttering trailed off as she reached for her hooded cloak.

Olga returned with their food and a small waist belt that she handed to Wynflaed.

"Tie for you, knife, drink," Olga gestured, as Wynflaed took the leather strap and tied it around her waist.

Very clever of Olga. He nodded his approval and went to his own belongings. He chose a slight, sheathed dagger she could hang from her belt, along with a drinking flask and eating knife.

"Resourceful thinking, Olga. Keep this dagger at your waist for your protection, Wynflaed."

Wynflaed took the dagger without hesitation and balanced the weight in her hand.

"I would not say I have much skill, but how hard could it be? Stab them with the pointy end until you see blood?" she asked with a cheeky grin.

"That is about right, but I promise to do all I can so that you never need to pull the dagger, Elskling."

"I know, Torben, but I appreciate the dagger anyway. I never want to feel helpless again. What now? I am ready."

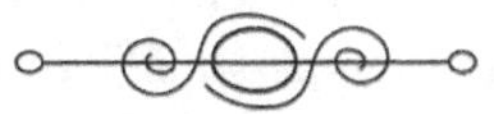

They rode side by side on their horses while Torben filled her in on his conversations with Ragnav, Leif, and Sven

"So, you think this Gunhilda helped her leave, the woman you were bedding?" He heard the annoyance in her voice, veiled but present, and he bit back his grin.

"Perhaps. We shall ask her and find out what she knows, and then we will continue on our way. This is her place, with all the goats."

It was a silly statement to make, no one would mistake the noise they made for anything but goats. The look of derision she threw him told him as much.

"I am familiar with the sound of bleating goats, Torben, but my many thanks for confirming it." Her tone was haughty as she reined in behind him when the path narrowed.

Gunhilda appeared in the doorway as they drew closer, leaning on the frame with an eyebrow raised.

"I was wondering when you would arrive."

The gall of this woman. He had half hoped she was not involved and had not betrayed him in this way.

"Gunhilda, your welcome leaves me less then pleased. From what you say, you have had a hand in Freydis running away," he challenged, while he dismounted his horse and walked over to assist Wynflaed.

"Do not be so sore, Torben. Freydis is a woman in her own right and asked for my secrecy," she retorted, but moved aside to allow them to enter. Torben observed Wynflaed as she eyed Gunhilda with a guarded stare. Gunhilda gestured them to sit down, and she poured them all mead.

"I do not wish to argue with you, Gunhilda. Klavik is my settlement, and I am Chieftain. This isn't a girlish secret Freydis has whispered to you. She has run away, and her life may be in danger. This is my sister!" Torben heard his voice become harsher with each word he spoke and Gunhilda flinched under his stare.

"You are right, Torben. I am sorry. Truly. I lost my good sense in the wake of my feelings about a certain situation." She glanced quickly at Wynflaed. Torben saw her remorse, but it did not cool his ire.

"We will talk more of this when I return. I cannot have my people working against me. Now, where did Freydis say she was going?"

"She did not say where exactly, just that she wanted to take control of her own destiny, her own fate. She asked me for a horse and directions to Stavanger."

"Stavanger?" he said in disbelief. That was a major trade port, ships came and went from all over.

"Yes, she was not here long, but she was resolute. She has been so unhappy, Torben."

He heard the pleading in her tone and ignored it, then turned to Wynflaed when she spoke.

"It is very curious that Freydis, who prefers to be alone and dislikes her scar being stared at, has ventured out so. Something more has led her to take this path, something or someone..." she trailed off. All of a sudden, she grabbed his hand with urgency. The moment they made eye contact the answer was clear.

"Guthred!" they exclaimed in horror.

A burning rage engulfed his senses and he lost control in a way he had not done since the battlefields. He threw the cup against the wall and roared his fury.

Beyond the haze of his rage, he saw Gunhilda and Wynflaed jump off their stools and heard the frantic hoofbeats of horses and goats alike. He stormed from the hut, sank down into a crouch, and grabbed his head as he fought for calm. He could not lose his reason now. He needed calm and focus to track down Freydis.

He felt two small hands squeeze his shoulders in comfort as Wynflaed's scent engulfed him. The lavender she drenched herself in and her womanly scent of sweetened honey and berries began to calm him.

"Are you back with me, Torben?" Wynflaed asked softly as she looked in his face.

"I am, Elskling, you ground me. I will never stop saying thanks to all the gods, especially Odin, in guiding me to you."

"What is our next move?"

"We mount our horses, we follow the trail I assume she is on, and we look for tracks and clues along the way. And hope we find her before any serious harm is done. Let us be on our way."

He gave Gunhilda one final glance.

"Gunhilda, Sven is taking charge, and I am sure he will come to visit you and have a similar conversation about your actions. I hope when I return we are back where we should be, because I will not allow this in my settlement again."

She nodded profusely as the truth of the action she had taken now settled in.

Torben ushered Wynflaed outside and assisted her onto her horse before he mounted Bein.

"We are leaving Klavik lands now, Wynflaed. Stay close to me, do not wander far, and obey any order I give you. This is not to control you, but to protect you in lands that are still foreign to you."

She must have heard the desperate plea in his voice as she gave no argument.

Chapter Twenty-Five

Unaccustomed to riding horses for such a long period, Wynflaed's buttocks were numb from her constant bouncing in the saddle. They had ridden till night fell, and she had done so without complaint no matter how sore her arse had gotten. She was distracted by the awe she felt when she watched Torben track Freydis's path using his skills and instincts. The route Gunhilda had given them was the main route with a shortcut overgrown with trees. Once Torben was confident the trail they followed was Freydis's, he took them on his own shortcut to cut her off. He had told Wynflaed there was a risk she would still beat them according to the indent of the hoof prints. She had been travelling at a gallop. He also spied an apple that had been nibbled on but not eaten to the core–the way Freydis ate her apples.

They alternated between a trot and gallop, and he pointed other things out to Wynflaed. Settlements to the east, mountains to the north, the furry flashes of various scurrying animals as they zoomed by. It was getting colder as well. Having lived in Northumbria, she was no stranger to the cold. But the cold here was different–instead of biting, the air was more like sharp little slaps. Only the skin on her face remained uncovered and that's where she felt it most. She found it invigorating instead of discomforting. The riding, however, she was done with. Thankfully, they would soon be setting up camp.

Torben found a spot for them to rest for the night, and she said a prayer to God, the gods, and any who would hear her. She needed to feel the solid earth under her feet. The spot he had chosen had soft grass that would feel nice underneath the furs, and there was a large rock formation with an overhang to keep them dry if the weather turned to rain. He even found a spot with a small stream, and she could not wait to splash cleansing water against her face. Too impatient to wait for him to help her down, she pulled off her gloves and hopped down off her horse.

"God's bones," she groaned loudly and grabbed her rear in pain.

"Wynflaed! You should have let me help you down, are you well? Did you injure yourself?" Torben asked in a panic as he rushed over and took hold of her.

"My arse is killing me!" she exclaimed without any care for manners and rubbed her fleshy posterior. She expected surprise or sympathy at her outburst. What she did not expect was for Torben to throw his golden head back and roar with laughter. Even the horses snorted and glanced their way at his reaction.

"What is so amusing, you pig?" she stormed over to him with a wince and pounded him on the chest.

"Wynflaed, Wynflaed, my sweet Wynflaed. That fiery, sharp tongue of yours never fails to make me smile," he said and pulled her towards him, so she pressed against his length. He removed his own gloves and moved his hands to cup her buttocks and gently massaged the flesh with his fingers. Relief spread through her extremities and mixed with erotic sensation as her body started to tingle.

"Ahhhh, ooooh," she groaned out loud and rubbed her face in his chest like a purring cat.

"Does that feel good, Elskling?" His voice was a raspy whisper. She could feel him hardening against her and she gyrated against him.

"It feels wonderful, Torben, your hands always do," she whispered back, her own voice husky as she reached up to kiss him, pulling his head down to meet her.

Their kiss was hot, wet, ravenous as their tongues mated in wild abandon. He kept one hand on her buttocks and the other firmly entangled in her hair. Two animals out in the woods. No sooner had she had the thought than Torben growled and tightened his grip in her hair, pulling her head back.

"I want you now."

With ease, he scooped her up and laid her down on the grass, peppering kisses down her neck as he lifted up her skirts with a demanding urgency. Feeling the same urgency, she moved her own hands eagerly to his pants and pulled them down until she had his pulsating shaft in her grasp. It was so quiet all she could hear was their rough breaths as they stimulated one another with their hands and their lips continued to mate frenziedly. The heavy coat at her back created a layer of warmth on the cold grass. Not that it mattered with the burning desire spread through her limbs. Their bodies still clothed, all that was exposed was their primal need. She did not know where she started and where he ended–they were one in mind, soul and body.

"Take me, Torben, take me now!" she demanded in a desperate plea.

She opened her legs wide to accommodate him, desperate to feel him at the centre of her core. He took hold of himself and roughly thrust inside her in one swift motion. A satisfied groan escaped him.

"We can be anywhere, Elskling, but when I am inside you, when I am with you, it feels like home," he whispered raggedly as he thrust deep inside her. She gripped his back, wanting all his weight on her as her legs tightened around his waist.

"I am yours, Torben. Always. You are my saviour. You are my home."

Chapter Twenty-Six

Torben lay on his side, Wynflaed still huddled against him in slumber. The fire was burning down to its last few embers and the birds sang their early morning songs. The night spent out here with Wynflaed, alone, had been bliss. The bond between them had been well and truly consummated, but it went beyond sexual gratification and genuine care. He was consumed by her – her strength, her beauty and her fiery spirit. As furious and afraid as it made him to be clueless about Freydis and her plight, having Wynflaed by his side gave him comfort. He felt her stir and looked down at her face.

"It gives me joy to wake up to your twinkling blue eyes." Her voice was soft with sleep as she cupped his stubbled cheek. He heard the scratching sound under her fingertips.

"I am in a need of a shave."

"No, I like how it feels, how it looks."

"If you keep giving me that look, I will take you again right now."

"I am willing, but you will need to feed me first."

"Apple, bread, and cheese now, then when we make it to

Stavanger I will buy you bowl after bowl of steaming hot stew." He pressed a kiss to her forehead.

They ate, tended to the horses, washed, and dressed. He appreciated her efficiency and lack of complaint until they went to mount the horses. He saw Wynflaed scowl at the saddle and held back a laugh.

"Come, Elskling, let me help you."

"Freydis had best be where we are headed because the longer this horse ride goes on, the sterner my tongue will become."

Torben held the reins of both their horses as they entered Stavanger. Many familiar faces smiled as they passed, and he nodded and smiled back. Curious eyes looked Wynflaed up and down. It must be odd for them to see him pass through without Ragnav and Leif at his side. He looked down at the top of her head. She held it high, the shiny tresses framed her face prettily as they poked out from her hood. The grace she carried herself with was a thing of beauty. Her soft but sure arm movements. Her strides long and commanding. Like a Valkyrie. All she needed was a helmet and shield. His fierce Wynflaed carried herself in such a regal manner.

"Torben, you promised me hot stew and I can smell hot stew." He watched her pert nose sniff the air and pull a face. "I inhaled too much, and it wasn't so pleasant."

Torben grinned at the face she made. Much of the trade of the port was fish, all kinds of fish packed in barrels and ice, but the smell was not so bad. It was the fishermen who carried the odour.

"Deep sea fishermen spend days working out on the seas, it is pungent work."

Her face remained pinched, and he could not help but chuckle.

"Let us get you fed before you lose that voracious appetite I admire so much." He tugged at a lock of her hair as he teased her. Once she was comfortable, he would start enquiring about Freydis.

Torben made eye contact with two young drengrs, and they quickly came over and took the reins of their horses, which allowed him and Wynflaed to enter a tavern without any delay. At this hour, the tavern only had a smattering of people and he eyed them all expertly, scanning for danger. It was mainly men nursing mugs of mead and steaming bowls of stew, except for one cloaked figure in the corner. All he could see was a hand. A fair, dainty, feminine hand. Wynflaed had followed his line of sight and gave a slight shake of her head.

"Good morn, two bowls of stew and some mead," she said brightly to the owner, who had come over to greet to them. Torben made small talk, discussing the weather and crops as he fought his urge to storm over and rip the cloak off the covered person. He knew it must be Freydis, but Wynflaed was giving him a stern look. He pinched the bridge of his nose and breathed deeply.

"Is something botherin' you, Chieftain Ulfson?" the owner asked him nervously.

Torben shook his head.

"All is well, friend, all is well."

As soon as he sat down, Wynflaed pounced on him with a firm whisper.

"It may or may not be her and if it is, we need to approach the situation calmly."

He threw his hands up in surrender.

"I will follow your lead, Elskling."

Wynflaed's lead entailed eating her stew and smiling around the room as if nothing was wrong. The frustration swelling inside him started to ebb as he saw Wynflaed's tact had worked to defuse what could have been a tense situation. He saw the dainty hand no longer clutched her mug tensely, but was relaxed. Torben looked to Wynflaed who gave him a cheeky wink.

"Now watch."

Wynflaed was proud of Torben when he relinquished all control in this situation. She had felt the fury and distress that radiated off his body once he realised the person might be Freydis. Wynflaed knew without a doubt that the cloaked person was Freydis by the way she used her free hand to twirl her blonde strands around her finger.

Wynflaed walked towards Freydis, sat on the stool opposite, and said her name softly. A few moments passed and just when she was about to say her name again, Freydis slowly turned. Wynflaed met the slightly sheepish but very stubborn face of her soon-to-be sister.

"Wynflaed, somehow I knew, deep in my bones, that you would find me before I made it too far," Freydis said wryly.

"Come now, Freydis, tell me what is wrong. What craziness possessed you to scurry off without a word, alone, into potential danger?" Wynflaed's increasingly loud rant trailed off when she saw tears shimmer in Freydis's eyes.

"Because you would have stopped me. Or Torben would have forbidden it. Ever since you told me about Guthred, I cannot tear my thoughts away from him. I want to go to him. My life is my own to choose, just like you got to choose. Why should my choices be taken away from me because my brother is my Chieftain?"

Wynflaed took fortifying breaths.

Freydis is young and naive. She lacks good sense but I've been presented with an opportunity to lead her back to sensibility.

"Come now, Freydis, you know that was a very different situation. Guthred took me captive and intended to sell me into slavery. Torben rescued me, Hilde, Cynewin, and Cola."

"I cannot believe he would do that, Freydis. How could a man I love do something so terrible?"

It slowly started to dawn on Wynflaed that Freydis's young infatuation had, over time, built Guthred up in her mind as a good man, and being told she could not have him had only fuelled this obsession.

She could feel Torben's piercing gaze boring into her. She turned and saw him walk towards them.

"Let's get back to Klavik and we can discuss everything at home."

"Home? How quickly you have adopted us all," Freydis accused her bitterly. She reserved her icy glare for Torben.

"Freydis, my patience with you has worn thin, and you will not speak to Wynflaed and I this way. Now come, we are heading home."

Wynflaed looked between the siblings and rolled her eyes.

"What an enjoyable journey home we are all in store for."

Chapter Twenty-Seven

Torben sighed with relief when they crossed the border into Klavik lands. The journey home had been spent in a stony silence, which Wynflaed had given up any attempt to mitigate. Instead, she rolled her eyes so deeply Torben had concerns over the stability of her slender neck from the exaggerated movement. He grinned when she mumbled to no one in particular about her arse being numb. He cast a glance at Freydis and saw her disposition remained unchanged. Head held high and chin jutted with wilful determination.

What can I expect? She is an Ulfson after all, he thought, as he recalled all the times his father had cursed his own pig-headedness.

Suddenly the energy shifted, so he lifted his right hand to halt Freydis and pulled his horse to a stop. A raven flew overhead then swooped down to eye level. It held Torben's gaze for a moment and squawked before it flew away.

"Torben, what is wrong? You are tense," Wynflaed whispered.

"I have a sense of foreboding. We must get back to the settlement now."

"Did the raven tell you that?" Wynflaed asked.

Torben squeezed his thighs and Bein began to sprint.

"A raven is a sign, Wynflaed, it can be good or it can be bad," Freydis shouted out to her, the hooves of her own horse pounding beside them.

"Whatever it is, when we arrive I expect you both to heed what I say," Torben shouted to them both even though he knew it was a futile comment, and he cast his eyes to the sky.

Odin, above all–protect them.

As they got closer to the settlement, three warriors rode up to greet them.

"What has happened, Vorund?"

"All is well for the moment. As a precaution, we have moved the people into the longhouses closer to town. It is Guthred. He arrived with a handful of men and says he only wants to talk. But he is asking after Freydis."

"For all that is holy, or not holy–I do not even know if I mean God or the gods when I curse now–will we ever be rid of this hateful Viking?" Wynflaed yelled angrily.

Freydis said hopefully, "Guthred? Has he come for me?"

"Freydis!" he and Wynflaed now shouted in unison.

"Vorund, keep the women safe and away. I am going to talk with Guthred."

"Women? Women?" Wynflaed yelled at Torben's retreating figure, as he spurred Bein on quickly.

Vorund stared at her. He kept opening his mouth, but no words came out. He waved his hands up and down in the air and, in any other instance, Wynflaed imagined this would be quite amusing. In this instance, she was furious. She and Torben were meant to be a team, unified in all ways!

"You are not going to be ordered about in this way, are you?" Freydis questioned from behind her. Wynflaed spun around so fast that her hair–grown out somewhat since Hilde had chopped it to protect her from Guthred–slapped her in the face.

"The irony!" she yelled, even though no one else would understand. Ha! And he was back.

"Freydis, do not think for a moment I am not wise to your true motives. But no, we shall not wait." She turned to Vorund.

"You said Guthred only has a few men?"

"Yes, yes, but the Chieftain said–"

Wynflaed halted his speech with the palm of her hand.

"Torben shall make his peace with my disobedience, I am sure we will have many more times like this in the future. Now let us go. Freydis, stay close to me and for all our sakes, keep yourself cloaked and just listen."

Wynflaed could hear Torben and Guthred slinging strong words at each other. She could not understand them all, but the vehement undertones were clear. They stood near the mouth of the bay where the ships docked. Guthred spied her first and that large, cold smile spread across his face. The one that did not meet his eyes.

"Torben, Torben, here is the lovely Wynflaed. I heard she

had returned to Klavik with you. The cold air and ocean spray agree with her."

She went to stand beside Torben and straightened up as tall as possible so her head reached the top of his shoulder.

"Why did I think you would listen to me, Elskling?" Torben muttered with exasperation but clasped her hand all the same.

"We are one, Torben. And I have an idea." Wynflaed squeezed his hand and turned to stare at Guthred. She met his sinister gaze unflinchingly.

"What are you doing here, Guthred?"

"This woman, she speaks for you?" He turned his gaze to Torben with lifted brows.

"She speaks for us both."

"Well then, Wynflaed," Guthred said slowly and turned his eyes back towards her, "I have come to renegotiate my marriage to the fair Freydis."

"That will not happen. Ever," Torben growled with a menacing step forward. Wynflaed squeezed his hand again.

"What makes you think Torben would ever agree? Or that Freydis would agree?" she asked him.

"Freydis and I have a soul connection, we have been fated by the gods themselves. And it is not Torben's decision or yours. You had a choice, did you not? Torben gave you options. Why does Freydis not get the same? Bring her here before me!" His voice had grown louder with each word, and he now pointed a finger to the ground in front of him. Demanding. Menacing. Wynflaed saw a raven out of the corner of her eye, watching her intently.

"You forgot the beginning of the story, Guthred. How I came to have these choices. Was it not you who ripped me from my homeland? Upon threat of death? And for what purpose except to sell my people and I as slaves?"

When all he did was shrug his shoulders and say, "It is the

way of the Viking," Wynflaed had to fight back the urge to furiously attack him.

"Then what Wynflaed speaks of is true?" Freydis spoke softly as she stepped forward, but everyone watching heard her.

"Freydis, my fair beauty," Guthred said in a syrupy tone with a sweeping bow. "How fortunate I am to gaze upon your beauty once again. Do not let what you have heard sway you, it is not how it seems. Your brother has done his best to keep us apart, and now his she-wolf–not even one of us–comes to stand between us."

"Guthred, in my heart of hearts I refused to believe any bad word spoken against you. I, too, believed we were fated by the gods."

Wynflaed searched her face for a sign that Freydis was coming to her senses. Her disillusion over this swine must come to a head now, otherwise it never would.

"Freydis, you are my sister, my blood, a piece of my heart." Torben spoke the words softly, but with gruffness, and Wynflaed's heart ached for him. Everyone waited for Freydis to speak. Only the tittering of birds and rustling wind could be heard. The energy she felt from Guthred was palpable and, whatever her choice, this could easily end in bloodshed.

"I have heard enough. I choose...I choose family. You are not who I thought you were, Guthred." He stepped forward and started to speak but stopped when he saw Ragnav and Leif step forward.

"I am sorry, Torben," she cried and ran to embrace her brother.

"Hush, all will be well," he said as he let go of Wynflaed's hand and moved Freydis behind him.

"You have your answer now. Your final answer. You will leave my lands, or we will settle this feud now, Guthred–you and I." Torben drew his sword and let it hang loosely at his side. Wynflaed's breath stuck in her throat when she saw Guthred move his hand to his axe, but then he stopped.

"I am not fool enough to fight you one-on-one, Torben 'Hel-Bringer' Ulfson. I shall go. But we shall meet again one day, my old friend. You, too, Wynflaed."

"Be gone with you, Guthred," Wynflaed said with a satisfied smile "You have lost."

Chapter Twenty-Eight

Torben stroked Wynflaed's shoulder, the soft skin warm under his caress. Days had passed since Guthred had unceremoniously been returned to his ship. In atonement, Freydis had worked tirelessly alongside Hilde and Cynewin to prepare for the wedding today.

My wedding to Wynflaed, my heart and soul.

In these quiet moments, early in the morning while she still slumbered, he said his silent thanks to Odin for the fate that had led him on this path. It had once been full of darkness and now it was full of light. He bent his head and kissed her forehead. He felt her stir and was unable to resist moving his hands down her silken body to find her wet heat.

"You are always ready for me, Elskling," he groaned as she ground against his hand.

"My body is always on fire, a fire only you can quell," she whispered huskily as she took hold of him in turn.

They held each other's gaze and breathed in each other's panting breaths while they brought one another to completion with their hands. The satisfaction of his release paled in comparison to the satisfaction of seeing the ecstasy that flushed across her face and escaped her lips.

"Happy wedding day, my beloved," she murmured and rubbed the tip of his nose with hers.

"Beloved? Is that what you shall call me, Elskling?"

"Yes, you are my beloved, my beloved Torben the Viking," she grinned cheekily. "Now tell me more about today."

Wynflaed had been learning their wedding customs. After the encounters with the ravens, she seemed to resonate with his beliefs. And he found himself a willing teacher to her curious student.

"We set the wedding on the day of Frigg, wife of Odin. She is the goddess of love and fertility, and we seek her blessing and honour her by holding it on this day. Soon we shall part ways, I will go with the men and you with the women to prepare for our union. Uh, for women this is to cleanse for your, uh, maidenhood." This drew laughter from her.

"That is certainly a moment passed, but you know how much I enjoy bathing. And what will you be doing?"

"I will prepare a sacrifice to Thor, the blood of a goat is customary. And I will also honour Odin. It is my belief he supported our union and aided our journey. I have seen many ravens since I met you. A non-believer would spew doubts, but I know the All-Father has been watching."

Wynflaed nodded.

"I agree, for I have seen the same. I was fated for you. Odin knew it as we do."

Some things would be missing from their ceremony, since Wynflaed had not come from another Norse family. And there had been no time to invite any guests from outside of Klavik since winter had started to settle in. This did not bother him or Wynflaed. They both agreed an intimate ceremony with the settlement was more symbolic. Their marriage was not for an alliance or other gain—only for love. And they would start their own traditions. He and Ragnav had retrieved one of their father's swords from his resting place and Torben would give it to Wynflaed, for their firstborn son. Freydis was preparing a bridal crown for Wynflaed, one their daughters could wear. It was bound with gold and silver and adorned with jewels–fit for the bride of a chieftain.

"You have gone quiet, my beloved, what is on your mind?"

"Good thoughts only. Our future. Our children."

"Guthred was right about one thing."

He grinned at the perfectly arched brow that rose in question. "He was?"

"Yes, in that you are a she-wolf. I can think of no one fiercer to raise our children and protect our family."

"It did bring me satisfaction that he recognised me as such, far from the feeble Northumbrian handmaid he took for a slave."

"If not for your clever plan to let Freydis realize the truth on her own, it may have ended very differently."

"My plan felt safe because I knew you would keep me safe, no matter where it led."

"Always."

There were three hard raps at the door.

"Torben, we are waiting for you. Put some clothes on," Ragnav yelled out, sounding almost melodic in his glee.

"Ragnav, do not be crude. He is right, though. Wynflaed, dress and come out here, we have things to do," Freydis added impatiently.

"I am still not sure we need to use so much of our winter stores on the feast," Leif said in his standard harried tone.

Torben pulled Wynflaed with him as he got out of the bed while the other three bickered outside the door.

"It is time, Wynflaed."

"Yes, it is, my Viking saviour."

Epilogue

Odin stretched out his arms for Hugin and Munin, who made their descent towards him. He trusted his ravens more than any other mortal or immortal beings. They took their places upon his forearms, and he closed his eyes to allow their memories and thoughts to settle in his mind. Odin had been looking forward to this event, the union of Torben to his Northumbrian sjelevenn–his soulmate–Wynflaed.

Their devotion to one another fascinated him. It was pure and unadulterated, indestructible. Wynflaed was Torben's match in every way. Odin enjoyed her fierceness and bravery. He agreed with Torben, she would make a fine Valkyrie.

Hugin and Munin had perched themselves on wooden posts that overlooked the wedding altar.

Torben and Wynflaed faced each other, hands clasped. They spoke words of love and devotion. Heartfelt and fierce. He expected nothing less. The people of Klavik formed a line and took a branch of fir from the basket Freydis held and dipped it into the bowl of goat blood borne by Ragnav. They passed Torbren and Wynflaed and flicked the blood in blessing.

Odin turned his attention to Ragnav and Freydis. Their expressions held joy, but that joy did not quite mask the other emotions he could sense lurking beneath the surface. Ragnav, while truly happy for his older brother, hid envy–not jealousy or spite–just a deep yearning to find the same love for himself that Torben had with Wynflaed. Freydis, however, held a sadness tinged with despair. He felt her grief at love lost and her fear she would never feel that way again.

"Ahh, young Freydis, a beauty like you will find love wherever you choose to seek it," he murmured out loud.

"You are obsessed with the Ulfsons, my husband. Is the beauty of young Freydis the cause?" his wife asked him, a delicate brow arched sardonically.

"My dear Frigg, you know I only have eye for you, and look how they honour you today," He winked his eye at her. This drew a smile from her, and she turned back to eating her bowl of cherries.

"I, too, have a vested interest in Freydis," interjected Freyja, "and she will find love, I will make sure of it."

"And what of Ragnav?" asked Odin, as he turned to Thor, who polished his hammer.

"What of him?"

"Do you think you can guide his path to love before Freyja succeeds with Freydis?"

Frigg groaned. "Do not encourage them to compete, Odin."

"The challenge has been set, my dearest Frigg."

With that said, Odin threw his arms out and Hugin and Munin took flight to Midgard once again.

Author's Note for you, wonderful Reader

I aspire to write historical romance across many eras I am deeply passionate about. This passion leads to countless research and an outlet for all the information I've acquired over my years of being an inquisitive history nerd. My desire to learn about the past has always been insatiable. When the idea started to take shape, of Wynflaed and Torben I stepped outside myself and straight into the Viking Age! I admit to loving shows like Vikings, The Last Kingdom and I devoured Assassins Creed Valhalla. But I am well aware of the creative licence taken!

Writing Her Viking Saviour I heavily researched what living in Norway would have been like, the native flora and fauna, Norse customs and way of life. Mythology wise, while I was familiar with many things I also learned many things! Like the Norns, what delightful characters, the origins of the Silk Road and trade routes. It was still very easy to slip into modernisation, the number of times I wrote 'England'! Thank goodness for amazing editors!

Something new I learned that fascinated me was 'The Norns', the Norse goddesses of fate. The equivalent of 'The Moriae, the Greek spinners of fate were an unexpected treat! I had not planned any prologue and epilogue but once I discovered Urd, Verdandi and Skuld I pondered how I could this mystical element. I write historical romance, not fantasy and myth. But the idea kept evolving and it became clear how I could loosely tie in this element and not change the overall premise. It must have been fate!

About the Author

Forever reading, forever dreaming. And mainly, forever wishing I was dancing at a Regency Ball, drinking *uisge beatha* in a medieval Scottish keep, navigating a Norman-Saxon romance, or riding up on horseback into a Western town. Follow my writing journey, as one by one these stories will unfold. To be kept informed of new releases, updates, and most importantly to connect with any feedback or reviews, please sign up to my newsletter that can be found in this Linktree: https://linktr.ee/SteffySmithBooks ! As an indie author, I humbly ask you to leave a review on Goodreads and whichever platform you used to grab a copy of one of my books. Or feel free to reach out to me directly!

Steffy Smith xxx

Also by Steffy Smith

An English Garden *Georgian England*

A Marquess of Roses

An Earl of Bluebells (coming 2025)

A Viscount of Lavender (coming 2025)

A Baron of Thistles (coming 2026)

Highland Hearts *Medieval Scotland*

The Bonniest Lass in Scotland

Highland Heartbreaker

Book III (coming 2027)

Curves&Cravats *Regency England*

His Regency Goddess

Lore&Love Trilogy *Viking Age*

Her Viking Saviour

Spring Maiden (coming 2026)

Viking in Love (coming 2027)

www.ingramcontent.com/pod-product-compliance
Lightning Source LLC
Chambersburg PA
CBHW030411120726
47904CB00007B/2238